Mad, "I" Went

by Jeffrey Turboff

©2017 by Jeffrey Turboff

ISBN-10: 069294172x

ISBN-13: 978-0692941720

published by Woodsnake Media

"Whoever fights monsters should
see to it that in the process he
does not become a monster. And
when you look long into an abyss,
the abyss also looks into you."

- Friedrich Nietzsche

Mad, "I" Went

Mad, "I" Went

Mad, "I" Went

PART III

...ON COMPANY MONEY

now and forever

factors of 0 and 1

sound action

medium rare

bondage

orbit

id

quicksand

the moat

a koan

horticulture

the end

free fall

the castle grounds

her majesty's chariot awaits

invitation

Mad, "I" Went

PART IV

...IN THE ABYSS

.

Mad, "I" Went

Part I
...In My Sleep

in the beginning/release

I can no longer stop it . . . this madness. However, for the sake of accuracy, let us refer to it as anger, thus giving it a human touch and no longer diminishing the phenomenon by relegating it to the realm of the socially inept and those who would avoid your gaze.

There's something about the unexpurgated expression of emotion that is at once cathartic and self-indulgent. I think the fact is it is one because it is also the other . . . But I digress.

Why am I angry? Because I've been panned by the critics. "The scripting is great and the story line is excellent as well, but the execution of the central character is handled so amateurishly that this writer wonders if the casting director had been struck deaf and blind the day he chose the principal, and of the principal himself, if he had ever set a foot inside a theatre before being cast in the role." So everywhere I go, anyone who knows of my work is also aware of my approach to it. I have yet to find a single unbiased soul on the planet.

There are those who would change my modus operandi and those who will take me with a grain of salt and there are those who will simply take me . . . and having reopened that nagging old wound, they leave some salt in it. (I rub it in myself so as not to forget too easily.)

Now, having recognized it as nothing more extraordinary than emotion, what action am I to take? I shall try to feel it . . . however, I know that I won't be able to convince myself that I really felt it. Emotions are such a minuscule event; it's all the associations tied to them that make them seem so big, so important. Did you feel it with all your person? If not, you may not have felt it all. Pffh!

That was Horace's final journal entry before his release from Mumford hospital. His release papers stated, among other things, that

Horace's affect is no longer blunted and he can speak at length about his feelings if requested. His eye contact is good. He has a strong sense of identity and reports that he is eager to enter the job market. His appetite for food and sex are at appropriate levels and he no longer has suicidal ideation. Horace still exhibits evidence of mild psychosis, especially magical thinking, but the symptoms are in remission and may not present any problem if he continues his medication on a routine basis. The discontinuation of anti-psychotic drugs for this patient would be disruptive, but probably not life-threatening. Released March 21, 1992 into the custody of the patient's father, Oswald Cyrus.

The release order was signed in ink in a fairly legible hand by S.T. Franklin, M.D., notarized by the front desk receptionist for five dollars to be added as usual to her monthly paycheck, sealed inside a large manila envelope with some other routine documents and sent off to the appropriate state agency. Horace was given his shoelaces and other personal effects and left the compound after a dinner of spaghetti and meatballs, green beans, rolls with margarine, and skim milk.

Horace's impact

Horace had the kind of face that looked instantly familiar. In men, the effect of this was either that they wanted to punch him or ask him an interminable string of questions. Women often felt violated when they would detect his gaze, and married women found themselves aware of their wedding bands. Most people checked themselves to discover if their behavior betrayed their sense of unease. Hassled by panhandlers, feared by the old, watched by shopkeepers, suspected by husbands, noticed by police, coveted by religious cults, haunted by federal gumshoes, and sung to by angels; each was an irrational yet irresistible reaction.

He was somewhat aware of the effect he had on people; that is, he was constantly aware in the presence of others that either he was self-conscious or he was making someone self-conscious. His usual coping mechanism was either to be sure to go unnoticed or to do something utterly human to allay one's fears (like cursing or catching cold). Of the two, the former made Horace feel shifty, and the latter made him feel like a buffoon. For those who maintained an ongoing relationship with him, he was hopelessly inscrutable, he was a simpleton and a fool, or he was a lover.

the garden – a still life

"Mangoes for breakfast?" the brunette asked.

"I like oatmeal," said Horace.

"How 'bout oatmeal with mangoes?"

"Hmm, okay."

She had the kind of face a man might not notice until another man had already taken the initiative. As she walked across the cool tiles of her kitchen, Horace watched her feet and the thought occurred to him that if she stepped just right, she could cause an earthquake halfway around the world. Maybe somewhere where they grow mangoes. Her feet seemed larger without the shoes on, and although the toes were the right size and not too clubby, and the nails were neatly trimmed and painted, he could not help becoming disappointed with their size.

Last night when he had met her at The Easyl, she had attracted a group of mainly homosexual men who were complimenting her on a 6' x 10' painting she called "Still Life", in which the body of a victim of civil warfare in some unspecified third world country was enveloped by glistening labia. She was smiling easily and telling them that the women's rights movement had to take the back seat for now, at least until there was some significant improvement in human rights.

"It's not uncommon," she told them, "for this country to give money to nations whom we are denouncing at the U. N. for unspeakable violations."

Horace asked her about the punch and her flock had scattered.

She brought him home on the condition that he would be gone in the morning, but he didn't talk very much, so she decided to let him stay on a while. She had a theory that said a person only gets so many words per day and then his welcome is worn out. So far, Horace had already saved up a week's worth.

exit the fig leaf

He and Sarah had been naked for four days by the time they ran out of fruit and milk.

"Fuck me! Fuck me hard! Oh do it! I want your cum right now!" Sarah reached for the remote control to turn off the sound on her TV.

Watching porn movies had made Horace very aroused. Sarah wondered if they would do it again. Horace knew they would. Neither had seen the picture before. Both knew what the final result would be. That's the thing about this kind of storytelling — a climax is a climax is a climax. Horace ejected the tape and inserted something else. Sarah wondered how much longer she'd have to wait.

Oswald's dream

It seemed like forever. The command was sent ten, maybe twelve seconds ago, yet the punch still had not landed. Apparently the arm never received the message. He looked at the arm and saw that it was in fact moving, albeit slowly and clumsily, the way one moves a leg to the floor to start the blood circulation once it has fallen asleep.

If I can't get it to move any faster than this, Oswald thought, I'll be dead soon; from . . . what was it? Suffocation? Strangulation to be specific. Where will it stop? When it lands, into whose face will it be crashing? Who's strangling me? Cannot focus on the face. Somehow distorted; rippled. Like heat waves seen bouncing off a distant stretch of pavement. Yes, like that, but not quite, because here were the waves, but without the heat. Underwater! I'm underwater! And suddenly the ripples cease and the face of his foe, whose hands are grasped tightly around Oswald's throat, strangling him and holding him under, comes into focus. It is Horace . . . his own flesh and blood. The face then disappears and is quickly replaced by a rapidly changing series of faces. First a cherubic infant which he inherently knows is his own image. Then his mother appears softly focused with light seeping out from all sides of her head until her face is silhouetted and the light, blindingly bright, swallows her face and Oswald feels the tears welling up in his eyes. The explosion of light subsides to reveal the head of a bull with thick muscular jaws, head slightly lowered, looking through large coal-black eyes. And now, gaze locked in gaze, Oswald's entire self is absorbed into and annihilated within those eyes. At once he understands what the bull feels when he sees the red flag being waved. Olé. That flag is reflected in the bull's eye and Oswald knows that now the punch must land. His own father's face appears and takes possession of the eyes, which now have grown flashbulb-red. A smile which says nothing if not "cheese" appears just inches below.

The smile cracks under the force of the blow, strengthened by all that waiting. Knuckles now bloody, cut by broken fragments of tooth, the punches now land in rapid succession. From left and from right. He sees the once handsome face of Horace change, becoming more hideous and distorted each time a fist lands there.

Still unable to take a breath, he cannot help, nonetheless, but form his own smile. No longer cherubic, nurturing, or obstinate, the face with the red-pit eyes begins to scream. The sound is a relief. A sound Oswald has waited to hear for a very long time. The scream is of extremely long duration. Exquisite. Soon I will inhale and this nightmare will be over. Longer than a man should have breath with which to scream. Too long in fact.

Mouth full of pillow, Oswald awakens. He shuts off the alarm and walks purposefully to the bathroom, his dick mechanically stiffened in response to the urgent need to urinate. Today it's gonna be different . . . somehow. The smell of coffee and urine - the taste of blood.

the red and the black

It was the moment she had waited for. He had promised to leave and yet here he was, positioned below her, subservient. She had never been happier until she had heard him say it.

"Okay, I'll do as you wish."

And since then, she could not have been happier unless he were actually executing it. The room had fallen deathly silent and there were no more animal sounds save those of Horace enjoying his gruesome cocktail. The thought that he might follow through on such a promise without a moment's hesitation only served to heighten her awareness that it was she who was calling the shots. If she wanted him to leave, he would be gone. If she wanted him as a sexual slave, she would have satisfaction. If she wanted an exterminator, then rid of vermin she would be. The occasional pit-pat of sacrament on hardwood made Sarah cringe even while waves of pleasure assaulted her every nerve ending.

"Still, life," she thought spastically, "ought to be this simple."

Oswald's final day

Is nothing sacred anymore? For Christ's sake, I'm trying to have some breakfast here, Iris! Can't it wait?"

Realizing Oswald would not be pleasing this morning, she took her leg off the chair and tied her robe closed.

His day had started off frighteningly enough with that outrageous nightmare, but to then wake up to bleeding gums, and finally to see his wife begin a new cycle right before his very eyes – he had thought upon awakening this morning that he would not dwell upon his imminent demise, but here were three omens within a span of as many minutes, each amounting to, at best, a temporally random component of a coincidental phenomenon, and at worst an attack of the rearguard, rightguard and leftguard acting synergistically to surgically cordon off Oswald's life-force as the next logical step in this cosmic conspiracy to usurp power either at its source or, failing that, wherever it may be found. Whatever the case, his appetite was waning.

exit Michael

The lack of blood, combined with the abundance of melanin gave the skin an ashen hue rather than the bluish tint so typical of those of Caucasoid descent. Michael appeared to Horace as if in some horrific dream. His belly was completely empty and sloped in concave fashion from sternum to navel, exaggerating the height and breadth of the chest. One could nearly see it rise and fall. Horace thought his friend looked much thinner, and then realized why: he had not eaten in three days. Michael's lips were far enough apart to qualify him to be smiling or perhaps in the midst of forming a smile, if only they hadn't been stuck together. Just a little dab of saliva between those lips would make them look so much more natural, but his tongue was already dystrophic and could not reasonably be expected to produce any, barring some diabolical miracle.

The man was rotting before his very eyes. Horace wondered how long it took before the corpse began to stink the stink of death, so distinctly different from the stench emitted by the living. Four days? Five? Was timing of the essence to the undertaker? No, certainly the embalming fluid would allow ample time to invite the whole family. A week if necessary. Ten days at the outside.

Three days of beard growth, the makeup, some embalming fluid and stillness. They have hijacked this vessel where once reigned razor burn, sweat, breath, and an icy stare. No more shitting, crying, cumming or driving; just the simple act of rotting. Even in death, Horace thought, we are disallowed a natural course. Delayed from reentering the food chain – by the casket and the preservatives – Horace's friend is lowered into the once-green earth with the aid of rope and blocks, pulleys and tears. An old black spiritual burns its way into Horace's memory.

enter Oswald

The trip back from the cemetery was not as long as Horace would have liked. It never is. It wasn't ten days ago when his friend Michael had been buried and it wasn't today when he saw his father lowered into the plot.

His father hadn't so much died as retreated from life. Oh, he still went through all the motions: going to all the right social functions, having sex with his wife, setting off bug bombs and generally living the kind of life which, to many, dreams are made of, but those around him – his coworkers and his wife – noticed in him a change during those last days. He seemed to be on the run from something. He had a frightened look in his eyes: frightened and bewildered, the way one looks when one has woken from a nightmare.

All his life, Oswald had kept a look of certainty on his face: unwavering stability which effectively masked, one might conjecture, an underlying fear of humankind. The one lesson he had taught his son Horace which he knew would outlive him and the little bastard both was that the only goal worth striving toward was disillusionment. He would constantly reprimand those about whom he cared to "wake up", no matter what state they were in: washing, eating, reading – he would even go so far as to lean over a slumbering loved one to gently whisper his plea: any was a state worthy of the admonition.

As Horace veered his vehicle onto the interstate, he wondered what form Oswald would take in his next incarnation. Certainly he had lain to rest thousands of insects, dozens of rodents: rats, mice, bats, and Horace's pet gerbils Adam and Eve which had escaped their playpen into the larger world of the Cyrus home (they ate a manuscript work of Oswald's, a pamphlet comparing the recent discoveries of quantum physicists with the beliefs of ancient Egyptians), an ailing house cat, several wild boars, geese, ducks, quail, an eight-point buck, and even an enemy prisoner of war. But perhaps none of these actions indebted him enough to others to require his reentry onto the physical plane, and there was also the possibility, Horace considered, that it is impossible to return.

Alarmed, Horace's attention shifted back to the road he was on just in time to realize he had gone much farther than he had wanted to and watched the exit he had intended to use streaking past the window on the passenger side.

a puff of smoke/the Earth shaker

Undated journal entry:

I flicked the butt of the Chesterfield onto the ramp which I had intended to implement in egressing from the avenue upon which I was hurtling. I had quit smoking. Years of starting fires just under my proboscis, er . . . nose, had served to make me inflammable.

The fire had been kindled within me and there was nothing it would judge unworthy of consumption. This thought, er . . . knowledge jumped like an electrical spark from synapse to synapse millions and billions of times, was penetratingly cogitated, compared to competing constructs, criticized, denied, defied, deified and demonized. Egged on by the example of the moth, I could no longer endure and ended then and there my resolve to harbor antipathy against my keeper. I exhaled an effluvium of hatred and was rid of the pesky habit forever. A conflagration had been ignited in the twinkling of an eye.

Soon Horace was off the highway and parking his car in Sarah's garage – well not his car, but his to use and whomever he chose to loan it to. It was a rental, although Horace preferred to claim it was being leased to him. Whatever the case, Sarah was no longer waiting for him and he was hungry.

Not finding her outside and no longer himself content to wait for her – folly – he knocked at her door. It was so tightly secured that had she been home, and she may have been, she might not have heard, and if she had heard, and she may not have, she might have been disinclined to answer, for why does one shut one's door and array it with golden locks if not to discourage intruders? Yet she was home and had heard his knockings, which to her had seemed like the babbling of a newborn child. She opened the door and presented to Horace a pair of ripe mangoes which he gobbled ravenously and then fell asleep crying in her arms.

The upheaval he had experienced in the days recently past took their toll upon him only in dreamtime. He fancied he could fly and enter people's dreams and their daydreams, their thoughts and their very lives. Like some messianic folk hero he would point anyone he met there . . . to the fire which purifies the soul, seated in the deepest and darkest recesses of the Oversoul's blackest night, beneath the basest realm of the human psyche, where only those of a chthonic origin may dare to tread undogged by spectral fears which daunt even those of superhuman constitution from catching even the quickest, most cursory glance at their mirrored-self, shadow-being, double, or as Horace called it affectionately, the it-soul.

He fancied he could swim for hours at a time without surfacing for a breath. Thusly he would chase the minnows which were continuously swimming across the mouth of his favorite hiding place and taunt the sharks and rays and even Neptune himself would somehow be dragged kicking and screaming into the game until, becoming impatient, he would strike the ground with his staff, and only then would all the tomfoolery cease and Horace would awaken in the arms of a woman whose name he could not recall.

So it was when Horace had begun to fancy himself a conductor of both the state of men's souls and his own fate. He had met himself and recognized that there was nothing to fear . . . these are the times . . . Papa was a rolling stone.

Part II

...On Foot

enter Xenos/enter Horace

The man in her arms was heavy, as was his odor. She had not been able to awaken him although she had repeated his name mantra-like over a period of time which was beginning to seem like an eternity. When she had met him the night before, she had thought he was an important critic from Art Forum magazine or The New Yorker. Not only had his name seemed oddly familiar (although she couldn't be certain) but he had a way of carrying himself that was characteristic of influential critics.

Looking at his feet, he had entered the gallery. He watched them as they shuffled him toward the wine and cheeses. She had heard the shuffling and turned nearly completely around to see where it came from, half expecting to see her friend Michael who once several years ago shuffled into her life with that same walk, sobbing about an unrequited love. He would have told the same story to anyone who'd have listened. Michael had sobbed in her arms and Sarah was a sucker for a man who was in touch with that part of himself. She had cried in his arms the day he told her he would be committing himself to Mumford for observation and evaluation.

She watched Horace look up finally, after guzzling most of that initial glass of wine. He stared at a spot on her "Still Life" corresponding to what she thought was a well-placed clitoris, aesthetically speaking, licked the wine off his upper lip and drained his glass. Then he began looking at the people in the gallery, searching, it seemed to her, for someone he had come to meet, perhaps a colleague or a lover whom he had long ago taken and recently spurned. He was experiencing the pangs of regret, she imagined, when he parted her sea of admirers, Moses-like, asking her something . . . what? . . . about Sangria?

She took the drink from him and listened graciously as he told her what he saw in her "Still Life" and found to her surprise that he understood the message she had painted. There was something there that warranted further attention.

She could not know that days later, still in her tender clutches he would be having a nightmare in which she did not even exist. It was a Sunday, or perhaps it was the Fourth of July. Evident was the feeling of community. All over town television sets glowed to the likes of "60 Minutes", and throughout the neighborhood, embers burned themselves out in barbeque pits on either side of every street. It was time for a commercial and Horace turned to look at whom he thought would make a wonderful wife someday and found to his dismay someone completely alien. The features of his new companion had become reptilian . . . hideous. Pink flesh persisted over the eyes, on cheekbones and on jawbones, but otherwise a rough toad-like skin and body shape had taken over and seated itself in the lounger best situated for TV viewing of any seat in the house. Noticing this drastic change in his fiancée, Horace looked outside to see if the rest of the world had somehow also become topsy-turvy. The sky was greying rapidly and becoming darker by the second. People all over the neighborhood were pouring into the streets. Horace and his fiancée, the toad, did also. As they did, the sky began to be streaked with a crimson red and a quiet blanketed the area like that which is experienced in the eye of a hurricane. Vibrating through the dead air came not so much a sound but rather a feeling in the marrow of the bones. At once the attention of the entire throng was drawn skyward as a ship, for lack of a better term, blocked out the sky from the south end of the street moving northward. It had come within fifty feet of ground level and despite its over four hundred feet of smooth white length, had passed into and from the field of view in a noiseless second, trailing behind it only the slightest rush of wind.

The crowd was still looking northward when someone behind them shouted, "The Earth is inhabited by aliens!" As each turned to face the evidence of what they had suspected for a long while to be a truth which they would never be required to acknowledge, Horace saw men who were, simply put, a race of giants. They were eight to nine feet tall with flesh the color of boiled lobsters. They were garbed like sentries from the Roman Empire and spoke catachrestically. Each had a musty beard growing from his chin.

Horace tried with all his might, while the details were still fresh, to document the shape of their vessel, knowing that by doing so he would be able to send back these mighty colonists to that place, light years distant, from which they had emerged.

Single-minded, he continued to sleep.

enter Michael/the nature of sardines

It couldn't be drawn. It had gone by so quickly it almost didn't register at all. No matter how many times I drew it, it didn't come out right. Words failed me, and I them. I couldn't turn a phrase to save my life. Around me the dead ones kept piling up, one on top of the other. Their heads, which normally served to distinguish them from the others, had been removed and perhaps rallied into the mother ship where others would be synthesized from them. Their feet had been cut off, ankles bound tightly together, and each was stacked in neat little groups with others who had had a common purpose.

On each city block a vehicle had its seats removed, and the dash – more room to stack the bodies before covering them with oil or mustard or chili pepper sauce or beer or sour cream. The short ones were stacked in three layers per car, the bottom and top layers facing the passenger door, the middle layer facing the driver's side door. Medium sized people were stacked in two layers, and only the biggest people were arranged four to six per car. Convertibles were the preferred vehicle of choice because the tended to be easier to open, although they did force the portions to be somewhat smaller. Considered a rare delicacy was the endomorphic family of four packed in sea water in its own American built convertible sedan, particularly if there were a family dog which could be secreted into the trunk marinating in its own vomit.

Which reminded me of the first time I had seen Michael. He was at my feet, sacrificing his lunch. (Spaghetti. Green beans. Mangoes.) I had gut punched him, the nurses said. I had been complaining all day that Jesus Christ was alive and well and living out his worst nightmare by coming to Mumford; that Confucius had so baffled me that I no longer remembered how to ride a bicycle; that Mohammed, when he finally arrived, would see to it that gravity no longer affected me, so when they brought him in, I naturally assumed the worst.

After I had oriented him to respond to the situation the way I felt like responding but never did because I wanted to get out soon, and puking as you know is much more unacceptable than violent aggression, I asked him why he had been brought here and he told me he had come under his own power and began to babble ejaculations about white being the color of death; sperm and mother's milk and hospital walls and the President's house, and it's always a white light at the end of a tunnel, the color of cocaine and crack, the color of the conquering horseman's steed in Revelations, the color worn at funerals in China and weddings here, it's the color in their eyes which you wait to see before you begin shooting, the color of little lies, and the color worn by heroes, and it was the color of the ship which would bring our colonists from a distant star.

"They can't be faulted for wanting to come here and slaughter us. It's their destiny, their conscience told them, to colonize all the way to the innermost arm of the galaxy, even if this means pushing us off the planet which most of us consider our home. White is the color you get when you mix all the colors together." He then got really dizzy and weak and passed out on the cool white tiles of the sanitarium's dayroom floor, chipping a religiously brushed incisor during the fall, leaving a small gathering of fragments there on the floor to break up the monotony of his sanguinary hysterics. Of course I didn't believe a word he said and now I know better. He hadn't slept with her. Me? I had done it.

After it was determined that I was not a danger to anyone,

they let me go wherever I wanted. The first thing I did afterwards was go look for sardines, which they didn't serve at the hospital, because the tins tend to have sharp edges. Sarah knew what it was like – that's what must have attracted me to her. She could always provide me with what I craved. There was nothing in the hospital which satisfied my need. Within the cold white walls of Mumford, one could find nourishment to be sure, but nothing approaching the gustatory subtlety of triple packed pilchard. Ahh, heaven!

dragonfly telepathy

That moment just after an orgasm was the one in which Horace's thinking was at its clearest. He realized that he would never see his father again, even while dreaming. He had died a death of which books are written – a tiny death – which ended in a whimper and left Horace satisfied down to the very base of his spine. Sarah idly fingered Horace's scrotum and his mind began to wander.

He remembered the day his father was buried and the odd occurrence during the short stroll from the parking lot to the gravesite, in which he learned about dragonfly telepathy. The dragonfly is a creature unique in its psychic impact upon the human; its size makes it impossible to ignore. It always produced in Horace an awkward mixture of emotions. Sarah was licking his navel in a slow circular pattern. He could smell the sweet aroma of her arousal wafting toward him from nearby. She began making soft smacking noises with her mouth and pressing herself onto his shin for stimulation.

At once he would be mesmerized by the grace of its movement and spectacular color, yet also somehow revolted – after all, this was an insect as large as a toad. He would react toward it with a little healthy fear and respect. Seeing it hovering there just in front of him he knew it would not harm him but nonetheless he would always wait for one to change its location before proceeding through. Sarah presented herself to be eaten while fellating softly and slowly Horace's already sticky member.

That was something that had always intrigued him. How a creature that substantial with no apparent natural defenses could afford to simply ignore a person about to walk smack-dab into it. They had an aloofness that extended not only toward humans but also toward each other. They would not even extend the courtesy of buzzing. An absolute refusal to communicate. They had begun to develop a rhythm together.

Other creatures had readily apparent methods of discourse. Birds chirp, cats meow, dogs bark, cows low, ants tap each other on the head, hyenas laugh, frogs croak, asses bray, and even humans had occasion to communicate by nods and winks, tics and grunts, coughs and farts. But among dragonflies – simultaneous orgasm – it was the movement itself which conveyed meaning; hence telepathy.

As he lay there catching his breath and wiping his chin on the thigh of a spent Sarah who was lazily rolling his limp prick around in her mouth hoping to extract another pearl of tiny deaths, Horace realized that he had never seen a dragonfly's shit. He imagined that if he ever did, it would most definitely be transparent. The kind of shit you can see straight through. Anything with that clear of a head would have to have something equally as clear coming out of its ass. One could perform copromancy on the clear acrylic shit of a dragonfly, revealing not an aesthetically pleasing meal of mangoes, but rather the ruthless precision of carnivorism; a perfect preyer; constantly debugging its environment with a detachment, inscrutability of method, swiftness and grace typically found only in the ranks of those who deal in three card monte.

monument to words

The thing I like about art is its adaptability, its disposability, its odor, its table manners, the way it stands with arms akimbo, the clothes that it wears; Jehovah, Michelangelo, Picasso, Warhol. Sometimes I think it wears too many trinkets: celluloid, magnetic oxide, oil on canvas. No siree . . . just give me words, and lots of them. Words like axiomatic proposition: internodal sympathetic predisposition; antonymously, gobbledygook, unmitigated segregation. I asked for a pen the breadth of one hair because I wanted to write down all my words all at once onto a postage stamp, so I could lick it and stick it to an envelope and send it to you, devoid of contents. It would have been much easier to accomplish the task by architecture; I'd build a huge cathedral, a monument to words, to the Word, and people would walk through it and sacrifices would be made there, and other art forms could play out motifs within the confines of the four walls of my words, er...stamp, er...chapel. But the sign here in my place of worship (white like heaven) clearly states the rules. No working alone, no arc welding, no hyperbole, solipsism strictly forbidden, no hair splitting, dial 0 for assistance. I loathe the way wordsmithing demands precision. It's more akin to surgery than painting. The only splatter technique available to the writer comes from the number .357 soft lead weapon. The pen is mightier. Player's bet.

cosmological map/exit Mumford

My anger, er...yes, anger, had just about overtaken me there at the table with the others, playing . . . poker. I hardly knew her, Sarah. Funny, huh? The way television likes to equate lunacy with humor. And there on TV was my love affair with Sarah being depicted surreptitiously, on a soap opera – only the names had been changed to protect the innocent.

The etymology of lunacy is Latin, from luna, meaning moon, and the moon in the tarot deck represents dreams and deception. So it's no wonder that some folks in the sixties thought the moon landing was a hoax, and others thought those who believed it wasn't real were crazy. People once believed that little men lived on the moon.

"You are straying from the subject," the TV was talking to me.

"I will not reply to someone who's not really there," I replied.

"But she is there. In your mind, she is there. Tell me about your mother, Oedipus, er . . . Horace."

Iocasta instilled in Horace the burning desire to speak to the good doctor in the third person during outpatient visits.

"Sarah."

Yes, Sarah was in mind when he spoke of his mother, and Iocasta was completely anomalous. Horace complained to the good doctor how the TV was never turned off in the day room, not even once during his entire stay at Mumford. The aliens had been planting messages for nigh an half a century now, and believe you me, doc, that's no man-in-the-moon theory.

"Don't you want to talk about your origins? If you are a god, Horace, why don't you tell me about Osiris and Isis," the good doctor who wasn't there, didn't mock.

Horace would speak of gods, but not before he had offered up to his healer his entire cosmology.

"I want to join my father and friend."

"Do you speak as a god or a human, Horace?"

" 'Human,' said Horace."

"Good. Why do you want to die?"

"I must, and yet I cannot join them."

"You are getting better, Horace."

They were not joinable.

Words were leaving him.

When Horace was in Mumford contemplating his withdrawal, he realized that a good route out of his madness, er . . . whatever, would start with an accurate map of the terrain.

"Disregarding Alighieri," I began.

"I was touched once," I began.

"In a good way, or badly?"

"His Kundalini was stirred," said Horace.

"His or yours?" the good doctor asked.

"His," replied Horace.

"Did he want his Kundalini stirred?"

"I don't know. I didn't ask."

"But he touched you?"

"And his Kundalini was stirred."

"So both of you were aroused."

" 'Yes,' said Horace," said Horace.

"And then?"

"I proffered a divine union," my voice was waning.

"You preferred it?"

"Yes."

That was when the administrator walked in.

"That is why your pens and papers were taken away. That sort
of activity must be discouraged here."

"Sarah?"

"Naturally, a much better choice."

So first at the base of the pyramid is nature. At the second level is that which tends to go against nature, procreation. Third is the level of God, or if proffered, gods. Fourth is the demigods, in this case, writers – Dante, er . . . de Sade, Henry Miller, Umberto Eco, Kathy Acker, Mishima, Jim Morrison, John Barth, Roland Barthes, Baudrillard, Burroughs, Terrence Sellers and Crowley of late. Fifth is the level of secrets, and secrets revealed. Then the sixth, and the seventh. Eighth is the level of practical magic, masturbation, medicines, and television. Ninth is gnosis and hypnosis. Tenth is the dawning and breakfasts. Level eleven is the past, twelve present, and crowning all, the all-seeing "I".

" 'My voice was waning.' "

"And you found sex an acceptable alternative method of
communication?"

"I do," my voice was waning.

"Tearing your hair out is not a healthy demon . . ." the good
doctor faltered, " . . . stration of dissatisfaction, Horace."

"I wanted to write; my voice was waning."

"Neither was your attack on Michael upon his arrival. Why did
you want to hurt him?"

My voice was waning. The good doctor was waiting. He had no hair, er . . . "He had no hair."

"Did the two of you play poker together?"

" 'And his Kundalini was stirred,' said Horace."

The administrator finally spoke up, "Horace, I'm sorry. Your mother is gone."

Horace thought briefly of Sarah, " 'I want to join her, I muttered almost imperceptibly,' my voice was waning."

our lady

I sat down, resolved to write a book about myself, thinly
disguised as a fictional character, which I am not. "I have never
been in a mental institution," he would say.

He was reeling from the impact. She had been crushed when a 21" diagonal Zenith was
dropped on her from a height of several stories and now she was dead. The owner of said TV
in a moment of marital strife, picked up the set during a promotional announcement for a show
billing itself as, "...the craziest show on television since that crazy lady of comedy herself,
Lucille Ball, left the airwaves a quarter century ago. Don't miss the new Queen of craze, our
lady of lunacy..." and threw it at his wife. Like the spent butt of a cigarette, it sailed out the
window and found its target.

realm of possibilities

Horace was the kind of person who could spontaneously change gender. Not in the way that you might spontaneously buy a hat to wear, but more involuntarily, like spontaneous combustion. He wasn't actually able to do it, but he was the kind of person who could. That is to say "could" as in I "could" eat liver and onions, I "could" worship the cow as sacred, but not as in "I could eat a horse" or "I could sleep all day."

Rubbing his eyes, Horace considered his mother's departure, and thinking of his father, he realized it had been his fault. They had never been there for each other. The question had always been, "Who would be where for whom?" When one had a need, it was a certainty that one could be found in the cold.

> I had a character picked out and ready for action. What had I done with him? Or was it her? I could not remember where I had left my character. Where was it we had seen him last? I am preoccupied with thoughts of Sarah. I no longer understand my own character. I am sleepy. Dad would be proud.

There are yogis who ingest poison and survive. Mom and Dad were not yogis. Eye movement during sleep indicates dreaming. The feet become sore after a long walk. Michael rowed the boat ashore.

exorcism and other rituals

Hallelujah! Finally someone had spoken openly about the puberty of Christ. A hot topic among choirboys, but not a subject addressed often in formal settings or in writing. The question for Horace still remained however: if Christ possessed the soul of a person, uninvited of course, and began doing things that made His withdrawal desirable, who would you call to perform the exorcism?

A much easier question is this: In whose name would the exorcist cast out the soul of the Living Christ from the body and mind of the afflicted? What remained?

Ah, yes. Sarah. The name means princess; bride of the son of the king. Not unlike the bride of Frankenstein really, only we have read about her already. Does anyone really read anymore or do we simply watch the words like we watch TV, waiting for an image to jump out and grab our attention? Love. It was love that brought them together. Words create power; sound action. They would marry. Eventually. Actually only the ceremony remained. The rest had been done. It had been done before. Ancient history. The guests brought pearls. The bride and groom wanted oysters. The caterer served ham.

light/the greatest mystery

Light passes through me and I am a filter for the light which passes through me and yet even that light which passes through me is filtered. It is filtered before it reaches me and by the time it reaches me it is ancient. Light is filtered by time. I have no history. My futile attempts at establishing a character from my experiences are tantamount to claiming that my breathing consists of all the molecules I've ever inhaled. The protons, neutrons, electrons, quarks and so forth do not constitute my breathing, and my character is not composed of his, er. . . my experiences. Both examples are of course processes. My character is a process. If you ask what it is beyond that, you are entering a realm in which answers may be elliptical at best. Comet. Come to. Come to Papa. Good morning. Glad to see you're awake. I had a dream, Papa; a dream that I stopped breathing. Some day you will, son. Some day you will. Now come. Comet, er . . . come to the breakfast table. This is the First Breakfast, er . . .the first breakfast I've had since - Jesus - how long had it been? I guess I'll learn about the rest later. The rest was good. (Yawn) Good morning. Shall I pour the coffee? Yes, Mama, if you'd like. Do what you want. What do you want? It's hard. It's hard to know. To know you is to love, er . . . Sarah.

The greatest mystery of the universe – the penis. By the power invested in me, I withdraw the question. You may kiss the bride.

yogis/rayleigh scattering

There were times when Horace felt . . . what was it? Lonely? Homesick to be specific. It happened most often when he'd be in a car and the light from the sun would hit his eye. It was then he'd be reminded that we are stardust. Sometimes he'd imagine that the earth and everything on it were riding on a sub-microscopic particle-wave of light, and that the apparent vastness of the cosmos was an optical aberration, akin somewhat to the wide-angle distortion of a camera lens. If you hold up your finger near your eye it seems huge, and if you were able to train your eye by constant practice to focus on your finger there, you'd no longer be able to focus on it when it was held naturally at an arm's-length away from your eye. Who can look into the face of God and live? Who can look into the sun without going blind? Who knows what evil lurks in the hearts of men? Man, know thyself. Ye shall know the truth and the truth shall set you free. There are religious men, yogis perhaps, who in initiating themselves into the secret knowledge of the Godhead, look into themselves, past themselves, shedding ego, bypassing the sense of a coherent "me"; they look to the source of All, the source of "me", of "earth", of Tao, of the Trinity, and see that there is nothing there at the source. This is not nihilism, but rather renders nihilism pointless. All that is simply is. It is ultimately nothing because it is ultimately one thing – whether you wish to call it God, Nature, Tao, Sunbeam, Thoughtcrime, Mantra, Aleph, Omega, or what-not is irrelevant. The point is this; once you've seen it, you shall see nothing else. These yogis, er . . . yogis go blind because as an aid to this visualization process they sit lotus-style and stare into the sun, directly at the source of all that we are until they see that there is nothing but light, and for the rest of their lives they will see that light and nothing else. That which is darker than pure light no longer reaches their eyes. There is no reason to see the light reflecting off of you when we can see that which is being reflected. To him you are now evidence of the fact of Rayleigh scattering. Individual life and death become so much Doppler shifting.

Sarah's gift

Horace had found a job. He would be cleaning up after church services. He would be alone in the place of worship to do his work; work which no one else would do if not he. It was constant, back-breaking work almost 'round the clock, nearly every day, cleaning up after Christians. He liked Christ and especially the Virgin, but as for Christians, er . . . messy.

Sarah arose from the connubial bed, put on a beautiful, clean, white, fresh-smelling sun dress, and proceeded to go down to the church where Horace had taken up employment. She wanted not only to see him whom she loved, but also to perform a philanthropic act . . . to give something to the poor. Upon arriving at the church, she noticed a bum sleeping on the stoop. He was blocking the doorway and she would not be able to enter the house of the Lord without awakening him. He was a man in his thirties with long brown hair and beard. He hadn't bathed in several days at least, if his odor were any indication of such matters. He wore coveralls and had been wearing something atop his head, but it was now removed, having come off in his sleep.

Sarah knelt beside the man and looking around, felt safe enough to proceed through. She would be seen by no one but perhaps by him for whom she knelt. She took the zipper of the overalls between thumb and forefinger and began to tug slowly, smoothly, evenly, quietly unzipping the overalls. She checked for the man's reaction, but he continued to sleep. She reached into his pants and pulled out his small, dark, limp circumcised prick and his balls, and then the smell hit her, pungent and foul, like Parmesan cheese and moldy carpet, vile and strong, and yet unmistakably penile. The man did not move. Checking to see who might be looking in on her and seeing no one, she continued with unabated sense of purpose. She bent toward the man and took his limp prick into her mouth, hoping to clean off the filth before beginning her task in earnest. The man showed signs of stirring from his long slumber. He groaned. His prick grew. He lay his hands on her head.

She blew the bum and so was able to enter into the Holy Temple to see him to whom she had come to consider herself devoted. It was beautiful the way the light shone through and was filtered by the stained glass representation of Jesus Christ of Nazareth. He was glad he had come. He was glad to have been sleeping at the church. He was awake now and she had entered the house of God. She made a gift to the church as she had intended.

lightning strikes

Horace was easily impressed by evidence of the presence of God and rarely convinced of other's ability to perceive it. He remembered having once seen a tree just an hour or so after it had been struck by lightning. The tree was easily sixty feet tall and situated on a residential street on the shore of a dried-up creek bed just behind a low stone wall which served as a dam protecting the still-under-construction subdivisions from possible floods. The lightning had made a gash in the tree from its top down to a point about eight feet from the ground, revealing moist, white-meatish wood not so many rings from the center. A limb of roughly twelve feet in length lay in the street. Thousands of chips of wood, some charred, others not, had showered the entire area. Municipal crewmen populated the scene, orange cones authoritatively placed to seal off traffic. A man in a bucket on a crane worked on a flimsy limb with a chainsaw. Twenty others stood around doing nothing; some spoke into two-way radios, others smoked and laughed with their buddies. No one tried to move the big limb or sweep up the chips. A car covered with charred bits had a note pinned between the driver's side windshield and its wiper instructing the owner to contact the city about damages crewmen had made to the vehicle. Nowhere was it apparent that anyone recognized the pure and raw power of what had happened. No one was looking up at the tree. No one was stunned into silence. It seemed that no one even recognized that this was a beautiful and rare sight. A site of pure destruction, utterly natural, without malicious intent. Horace resented them their vulgarity, their disrespect. They treated this as commonly as any street repair, while Horace felt it was more like a car wreck. He could sense the shocking traumatic aspect of what the tree had undergone and felt it still reverberating in the roots under the pavement beneath his feet. He swept the last of the debris into a dustpan as Sarah entered the chapel stuffing a tissue into her purse. She stopped near the rearmost pew and took in the experience of the stained glass scenes depicting Jesus in his most glorious moments.

Emptying his dustpan, Horace said in a voice just louder than a whisper, "Mine eyes have seen the glory . . ."

"Mine too," said Sarah, snapping her purse shut.

They met at the altar and embraced.

tetragrammaton/lend me your ear

The Word . . . what was it? Sarah bent over and moved closer. Horace got a better angle on it. He wanted to know it and possess it, to understand it and make it his own. Sarah was enjoying the process of simply spending time and attention here, although she had to admit she did wish she knew a little more than she did now. There is a certain danger in learning too much too soon, however, and Sarah was willing to back away from the whole thing for awhile, go home, think it over for a while, take a bubble bath perhaps, and just wait to see if the issue had any staying power.

"Four letters."

"What?"

"It's a four letter word, " Horace said.

He pointed at each letter of the word individually as he counted off.

"See? One . . . two . . . threeee, right there . . ."

"Oh, yeah!"

"And four."

Each had been written permanently onto its impermanent canvas by the ancient art of tattoo, by someone who must have been an absolute master craftsman, for each letter was only a centimeter tall. The first two were placed along the anti-helix, the first at the top at 90°, the next at 180°, closest to the back of the head. The third was almost inside the ear, on the underside of the tragus, and the fourth was located at the very tip of the earlobe, normally visible only to midgets and those insects with the keenest of vision.

Looking up for a moment, Sarah thought about where she was, standing here on this stoop, looking across the church parking lot, and wondered how it was possible to be here doing what she was doing. She looked beyond the street with all its traffic – cars full of oblivious citizens driving to and fro – beyond them too, to the cemetery, with its neatly trimmed lawn punctuated by an occasional fresh mound of dirt. Hundreds of times the sign of the cross repeated every few yards. Each one a few feet above the head of an unrepentant sinner (or repentant as the case may be). Sarah began to feel that the church made absolutely no sense in the light of what she was experiencing right now. It was so beautiful to be here with her new husband, discovering mysteries together, and yet revulsion enveloped her as well when she considered the mysteries' nature. She felt a stirring in her loins.

"I'm going to touch it."

"No, don't! It's disgusting!"

Using his index finger, Horace nudged the ear, which was no longer attached to its precious owner. He shooed a fly. He wiped some blood off with his thumb. The letters were still very hard to discern.

"It's not in English."

"I'm gonna be sick."

"I love you, Sarah."

Sarah took a step off of the stoop where the man had lain not long ago and began purging and retching, coughing and spitting, trying to regain some sense of normalcy. Up came everything – this morning's breakfast as well as the Last Supper she had eaten. Everything the young couple had shared the previous midnight – the red wine, the pita bread, the goat cheese, everything.

"It's definitely not English. Are you alright, honey?"

"Mmmmph...Qoph."

"It's definitely not English and I'd say not even Indo-European at all."

Sarah spat twice, blew her nose and stood upright sniffing back something very awful tasting with a snort.

"It's Afro-Asiatic of some sort, and if I had to guess, I'd say..." He squinted to get a better look at the letters, which would almost fit through a needle's eye (they had already had to pass through a needle to get to the ear).

"Er . . . I'd say it's Chaldean."

"Chaldean? How do you know Chaldean?"

"I spent a lot of time looking at dictionaries as a kid."

Is he kidding, thought Sarah. Just then she noticed that the ear had changed slightly in appearance. It reflected more light than before, although the blood on it had now completely coagulated.

"Whoever had been attached to this ear must have been a very good listener. I think this person must have been very sympathetic." Horace was divining the man's past by studying the shape and folds of the ear; a dead art akin to phrenology or palmistry and more organic than I

Ching or tarot. It had obviously outlasted its usefulness.

"It's gold."

"Yes, it's definitely a rare find."

"No, look. It's gold. After you touched it, er . . . look at it."

"Sarah, nothing has changed. It's still a piece of meat with four Chaldean characters tattooed to it."

A low rumbling sound was heard in the distance.

Temporarily blinded by a light as brilliant as the sun, as a hundred suns, as a hundred million suns, Sarah and Horace grope for the familiar feel of each others' bodies, both momentarily uncertain where they are. As though in a beautiful dream, they find themselves naked, caressing one another's bodies with a precise sexual intuition till now unknown to either; ecstasy which could best be described in terms Tantric. Both feel as though they are inside a giant egg consisting of one continuous erogenous zone. Exploring each other by only the sense of touch, they feel as though they are floating at the surface of a primordial soup. It is Edenic. It is limitless, and so is their pleasure. The thin gauze which typically serves to separate a man from a woman, a husband from his wife, is rent and dissolves. Horace detects the faint metallic taste of blood on his palate. They begin to fuck. It seems to go on forever. Their rhythm is perfectly coordinated, then perfectly syncopated. It does go on forever. As the light subsides, Horace finds himself standing. He does not remember getting to his feet. He is fully clothed. A tall man with a very sunburnt back disappears into a strange vessel.

As he opens his mouth to yell out the man's name (Aladdin? Beelzebub? Phineas?) he notices something is in it. He reaches between his teeth and removes a communion wafer from his tongue, embossed with the words MALACHI 3.1-5. Turning to look at Sarah, he sees her in a similar state. The cite on the wafer in her mouth is PSALMS 94.1-9. Both immediately look down, still slightly dizzy from their recent endorphin surge, but the ear is gone. In its place is a salmon, bloated with roe, dead. Making a meal of this unlikely parting gift are nearly seven hundred flies which form a trail from the fish to the man entering the vessel. The hatch closes and the craft ascends and is gone in a second.

driving, dragonflies, and semiotics

We humans are at our most telepathic while driving, especially highway driving. We have to be; our language at sixty miles an hour is limited, as is our range of expression. There is no way to inflect the honking of a horn. There are no eyebrows on a turn signal. Flashing your brights, while perhaps meaningful, is as glib as spitting. It's as if driving were mankind's apology and atonement for the gift of speech. It puts us back on a level of communication equal to that of other animals. There is no singularity of expression in a car other than accidents or bumper stickers. Driving becomes a guessing game. Pure language.

The faster we drive, the closer we are to moving at the speed of thought. When we reach the speed of thought we become pure thought. Accidents tend to happen when we are close to home or driving at high speeds.

Dragonflies, while incommunicado vis-à-vis each other, do reach out to humans where we are most receptive, on the highway. They are great linguists. As a species, they are unsurpassed at semiotics.

They live life to the fullest and die beautifully playing a word game in which they gather at highways and ride the drafts, trying to get as close as possible to the cars. Proximity is an important contributor to effective communication. Sometimes they get too close.

Michael's dream

Holding his ear, Michael cried out for comfort. He asked Horace why he had kicked him in the head. Horace told him – it was because he wanted to be dead, and since they wouldn't let him die perhaps he would kill.

Michael replied with a story.

I had this dream where this old guy, a white guy, I mean old, old like 400 or 4000 or 400,000, he takes me on this walk through my life starting before I was born. He spins this huge wheel, cosmic, like the wheel of fortune card you know, like the tarot? and the thing, it comes to a stop and I can see my zodiac sign and then a sign about what religion I'm gonna be. Now this little space at the top of the wheel is starting to come full into view, and I see what the flag of my country looks like and what my gender is and how much money I'm gonna be born into and all this other shit and the whole time I'm zooming toward this part of the wheel and I just know I'm gonna fly right through it and I do and when I come out the other side I'm an infant and I've still got the umbilical cord attached to me and I'm hopin' and prayin' that they don't disconnect me from it 'cause it's like my lifeline to this old white guy and just as I'm thinkin' that, I get slapped on my ass and boom I'm alive and I'm cryin' my little black ass off because it's gonna be a long time till I see that old dude again, and my eyes can't see so good so I'm lookin' around the hospital room and I realize when I see my momma that I'm black, I'm gonna be black all my life, and by the time I'm dead I'm not even gonna wanna see that old dude and so now I'm tired and all I wanna do is sleep and Momma's holdin' me and I fall asleep. When I wake up I'm here on the ward and it's just as real as this is right now but I don't know why I'm following him, but I am, and he walks down the G-wing and makes a turn like he's going to H, but instead of that dayroom there's this motherfuckin' gallows! No shit. And he stops walkin' and we're just standin' there. And we're standin' there. And nobody's in any hurry. And I'm standin' there. And I look around and I can still feel him, but he's not there anymore. And there's nothin' else to do. So I start walkin' the stairs and I get on the first one and I can picture when my momma and poppa met. On the second step, I'm feeling what it was like when I was conceived, you know, what the fuck was like, how it felt to him, what was going through her mind, the funky smells and who slept on the wet spot and all that shit. On the third step I look back and that old dude is still gone, and by now I mean he's really gone, but I feel like I got to keep going, like I'll be some kind of asshole thief if I turn back now. On the fourth step there's all these Malcolm X's and Reverend Kings and DuBoises and Carvers and Tubmans and Jackie Robinsons and they're backing away from me up toward the top and I wanna see who else is there and I wanna join them so I go up a step, and so now I'm sittin' on the back of this motherfuckin' bus with a bunch of other brothers and shit, and all these starched white folks are sittin' up there ignorin' us like we're not there and I'm startin' to wonder if we are and then I wonder if I'm on this staircase for real and now I'm trippin' for real 'cause I can see that rope and I'm startin' to think, shit there's not that many steps left, but I take another anyway and this sixth step starts me thinkin' 'bout bein' in this hospital and I'm tryin' to figure out how come I didn't know about this gallows before and I'm in my mind walkin' all over the hospital tryin' to figure out where it is, thinkin', maybe I only thought it was down here by H-ward, and I'm walkin' all over, and it's like, shit, this can't be anywhere for real. This is bullshit and I know it's bullshit so I'm not worried at all and I wanna walk up all the rest of the steps fast and get it over with so I can prove it's bullshit, and so I get up to the seventh and I start thinkin' about that old white dude and for the first time in my life I'm thinkin' about him like he's the devil, like I always used to think he was God and like he was guiding me through life and shit and now for the first time I'm saying to myself what if that's wrong? What if he's takin' me for a ride, I mean shit I always trusted him but now I'm here and I'm six steps away from hangin' and I'm startin' to get this image of a lynch mob and I see that old dude look at me like c'mon you know me better than that and as soon as I let down my guard, like I'm thinkin', shit that's stupid, and right then, that's when he pulls his hood down and I can see these burning crosses reflected in his eyes through the slits in his hood and I start running, but I only make it to the eighth step and there's this room. It's real quiet. There's this TV set. So I turn it on and I'm watchin' my life. You know, I can see myself tying my shoes for the first time and learning to ride a bike and being sick staying home from school, graduation, getting laid, and all those days wasted on trying to make next month's rent, and now I'm under. I can't control shit and I wanna run back to the bottom of the stairs but like I said I'm under. I'm hypnotized and I step up to the ninth and I can feel my head breaking open, not like violent or anything but like a bird coming out of its egg, but my legs buckle and I'm on my knees and I guess the stairs moved under me 'cause I'm on the tenth and I'm thinkin', shit, I've done a lot of shit and it wasn't easy at all getting all the way up here where I am, but at the same time I'm thinkin' if I got all the way up here there must be a whole bunch of other steps that I got no hope of reaching, but I look up and there's just three and all this stuff starts comin' out of the top of my head, like a lobster crawls up there to the next step and keeps going and this fine looking white girl which she feels like she's me but she crawls outta me so now I can't figure out what's me anymore at all and then that wheel comes outta me too and it starts spinning and it's going around and it seems like it's spinning a long time and it's slowing down and it's starting to come to a stop and I see 11 go by, and then 12, and now I'm not Michael anymore, I'm just this vibe, right? and right when I see 13, I'm starting to see something coming into focus behind the number, whatever's next, you know, after Michael, and before I can focus completely on just what the fuck it is, the fuckin' nurse walks in and starts yellin' at me, "Michael, wake up. It's time to take your pill. Wake up, Michael . . . Michael . . . wake up."

"So what?" replied Horace.

"So don't fuck with me, alright?"

where angels fear to tread

Horace had visited where angels fear to tread. So who had he met there? You want to speak of the devil. Not so. There are eight other orders of spiritual beings above angels: archangels, principalities, powers, virtues, dominions, thrones, cherubim, and seraphim. In such a densely populated realm, one would think he'd have seen them. He would not have recognized them if he had. They had not seen him either. Yes, he had gone where angels fear to tread and had escaped unnoticed. He had entered a universe in which he was the only sentient being. When he first arrived there, it was an infinitely small, cramped space, smaller than the naked eye can grasp, and yet all of Horace's essence fit inside it and forced its expansion. He had fallen through a fissure in human consciousness which he both discovered and created and he entered a universe which both pre-existed his arrival and depended upon his presence for its existence, its sustenance, and its destruction. He felt guilty for bringing it into existence, as though he were throwing the natural order out of synch, but had it not existed without him? His guilt compelled him to try to destroy it as though everything would return to what it had been before this place came into being, but was it his to destroy? It was all inside him, contained within his consciousness, but did that give it any less of a right to exist? He wanted to sustain it. He feared its inevitable disappearance. Would it be sudden? How long could he keep it going? Which was more important – length or breadth, or was depth more important than either? He joked (to no one in particular) that he would begin referring to himself as an Abyssinian.

I had focused my energy for weeks on disappearing from my
quarters and reappearing as an alien emerging from a strange
vessel.

Would he know it if he achieved this goal? Would that not change one so much, create such a shock that he would no longer associate the pre-emergent being with that which comes out of a transplanetary craft? Would he survive such a change in essence? Perhaps it would be easier to learn to pass through solid matter than through time-space.

Confined to this body, I am a five. Five appendages – legs,

arms, head. And each five has a five of its own – five fingers, five toes, two nostrils two ears and a mouth. I am hemmed in by the tyranny of the three. Three points define a plane. Three dimensions.

In the spirit world, Jesus was attached to a pentacle in lieu of his shouting. When this image was mediated by a realm confined to three dimensions, the resultant image was the one which now predominates, in which four is the persistent message. And yet, because water seeks its own level, the fifth is insistent upon arising, even in this physical realm, resurrecting itself as it were. Thus we have the disproportionate Christian obsession with/repression of Martian concerns. I have one wish for this world . . . that Jesus might get some rest.

the shape of things to come

Narcoleptic goats have come into increasing popularity as household pets.

countdown

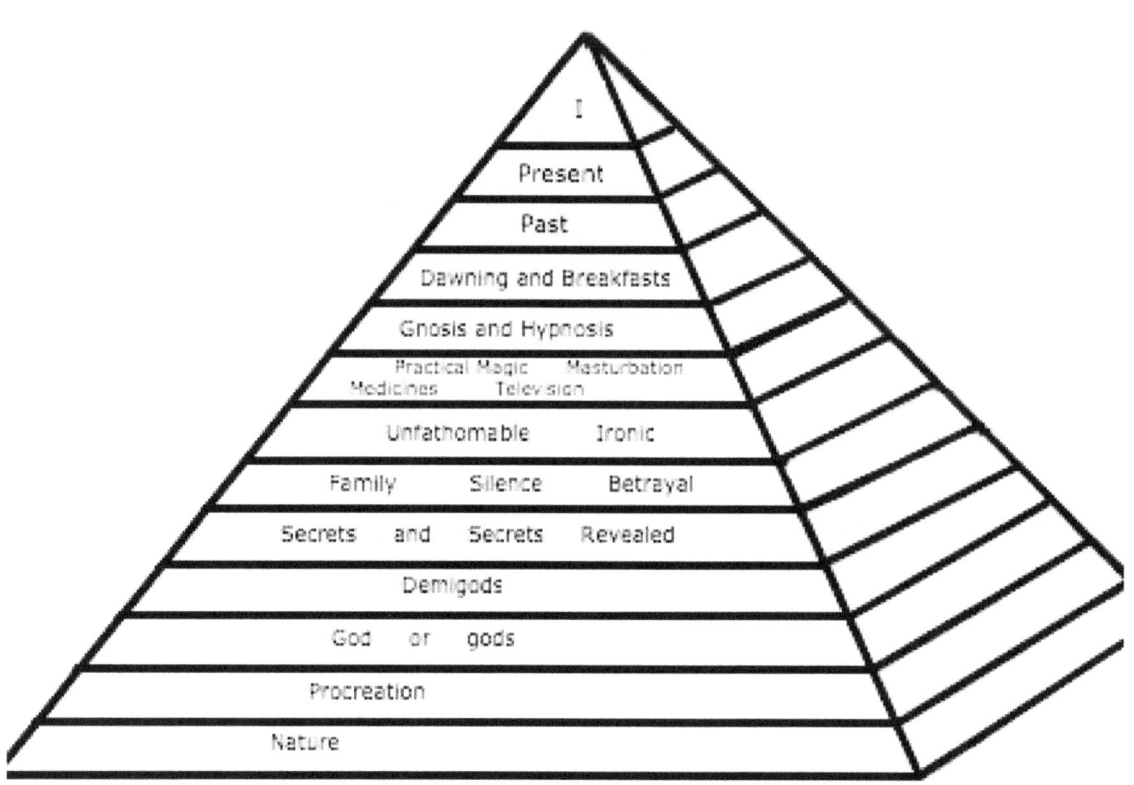

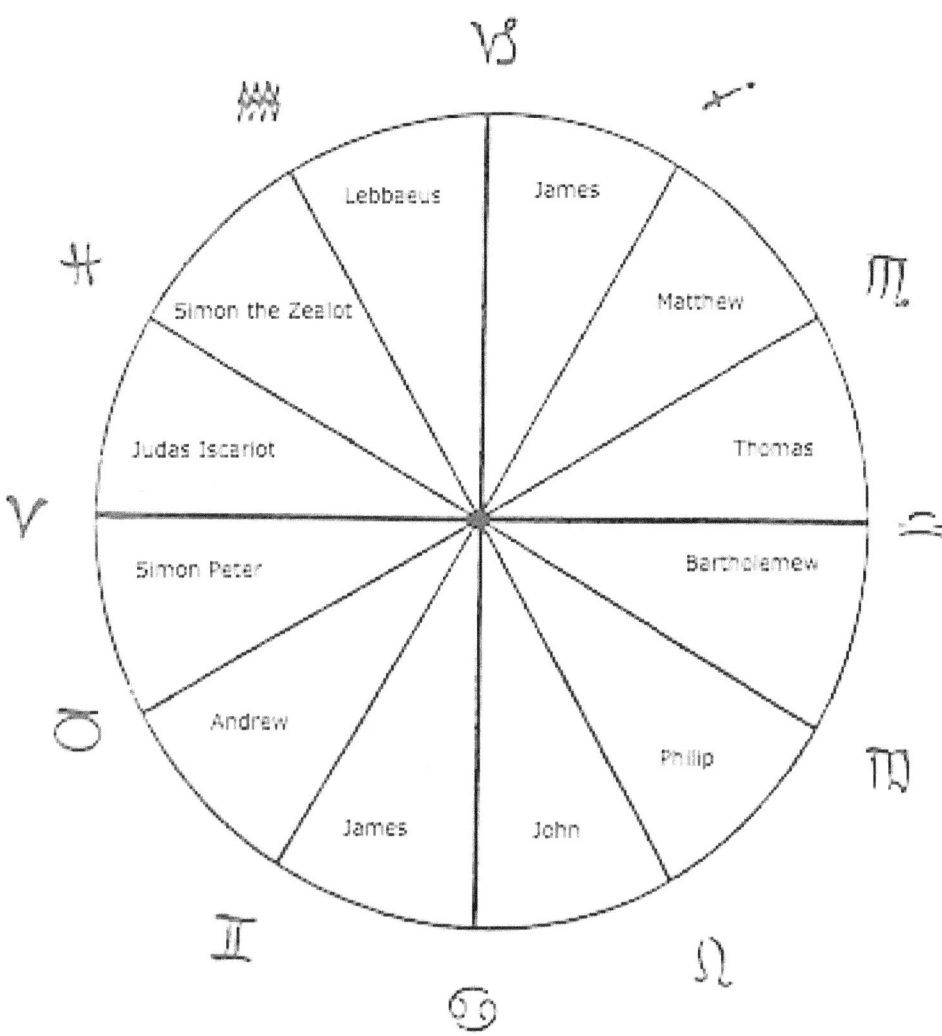

```
A B R A C A D A B R A
A B R A C A D A B R
A B R A C A D A B
A B R A C A D A
A B R A C A D
A B R A C A
A B R A C
A B R A
A B R
A B
A
```

Exodus 20.3-17

VIIII

l'Ermite

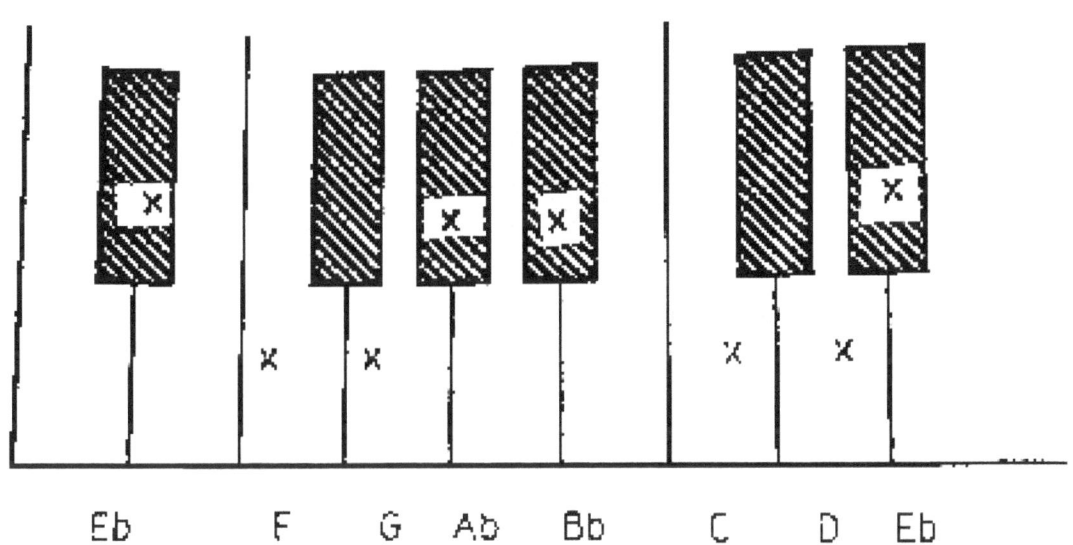

Eb   F   G   Ab   Bb   C   D   Eb

Journal

$13/7 = 1.857142$

$12/7 = 1.714285$

$11/7 = 1.571428$ dividing by

$10/7 = 1.428571$ seven

                         produces

$9/7 = 1.285714$ an irrational

$8/7 = 1.142857$ number

                         with the

$6/7 = 0.857142$

                         same sequence

$5/7 = 0.714285$ of repeating

$4/7 = 0.571428$ numbers.

$3/7 = 0.428571$

$2/7 = 0.285714$

$1/7 = 0.142857$

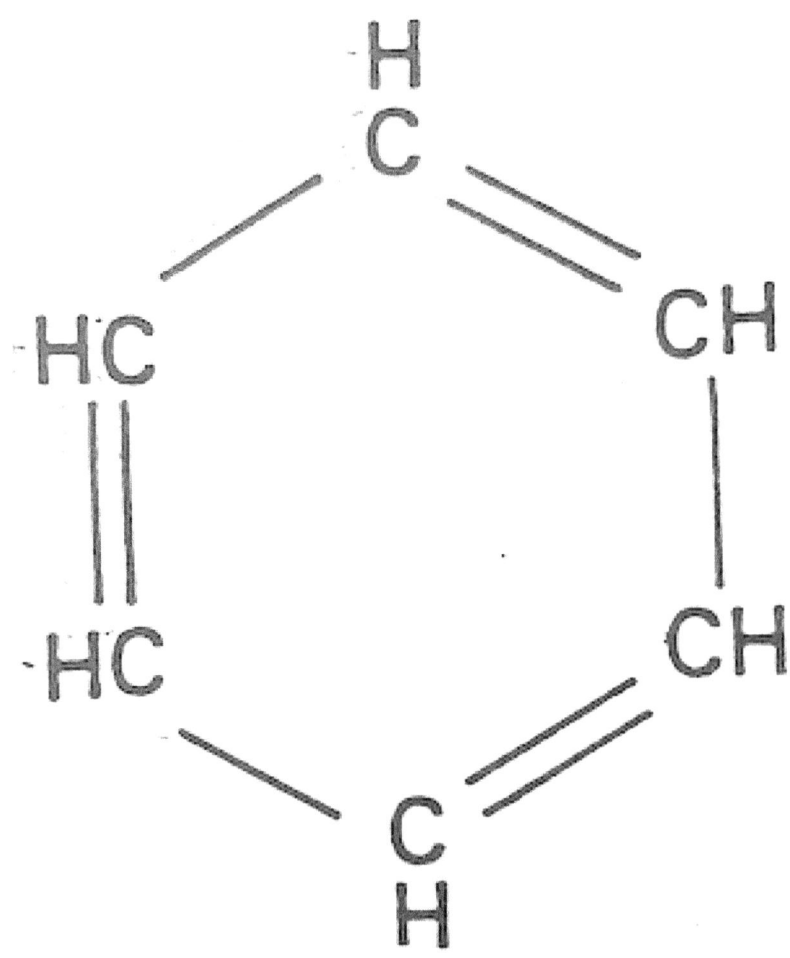

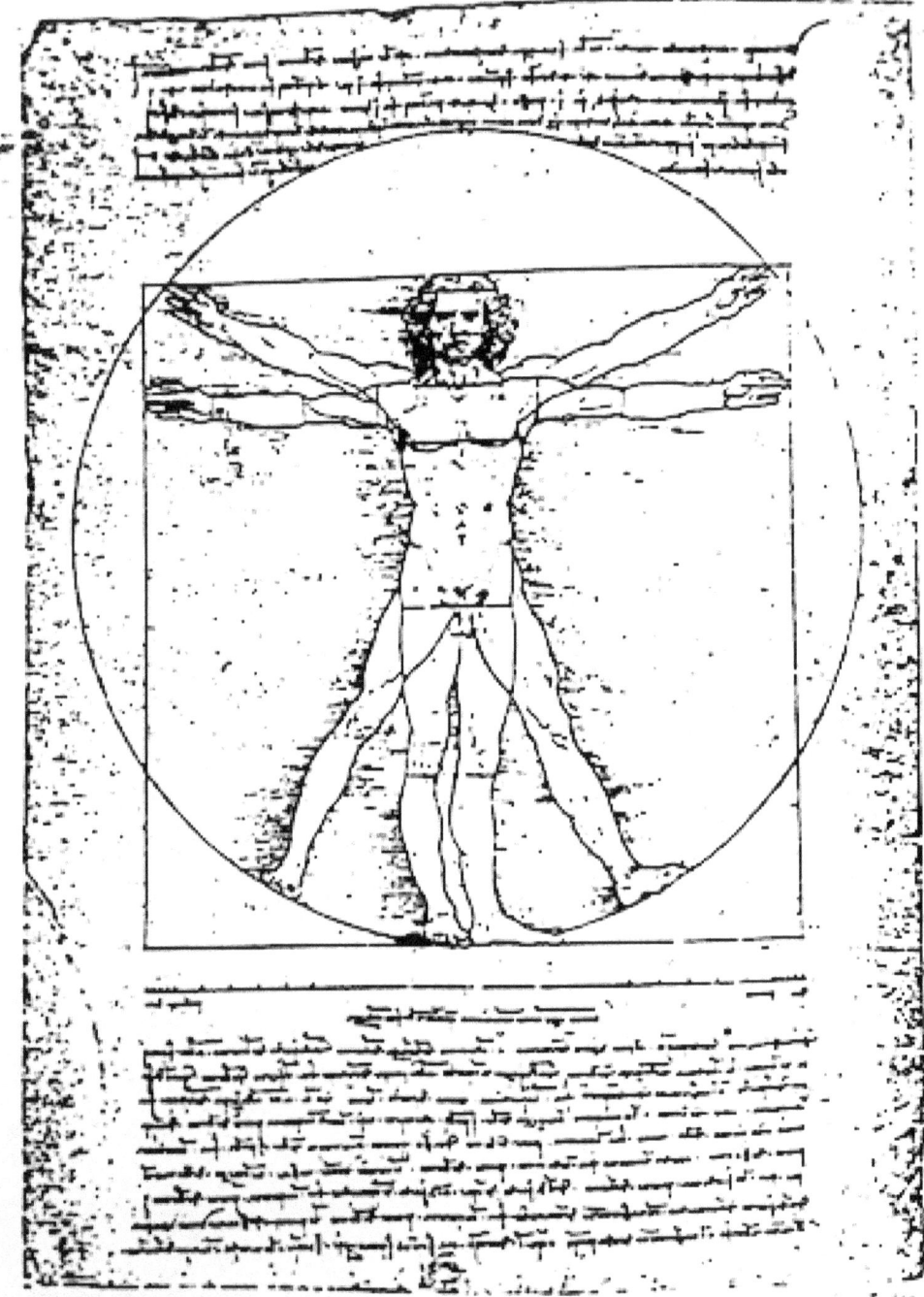

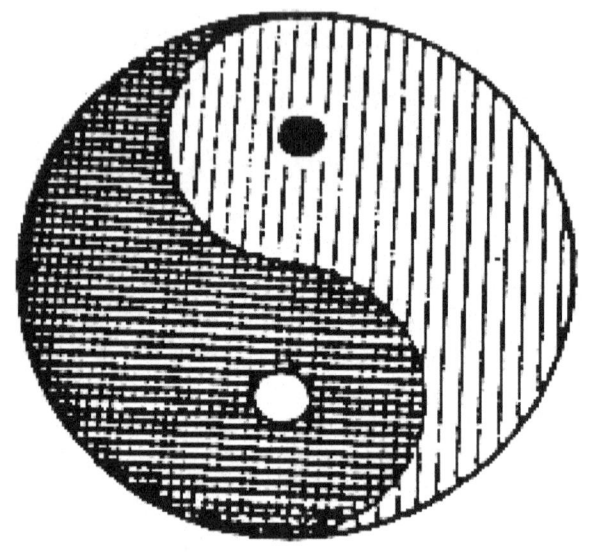

Nature first begets one thing.

Then one thing begets another.

The two produce a third.

In this way, all things are begotten.

Why? Because all things are impregnated by two alternating tendencies, the tendency toward completion and the tendency toward initiation, which, acting together, complement each other marginalia

Horace awoke one afternoon from a drug-induced nap and wrote the following thoughts in his journal while his mind still had a dreamy quality:

It was done. It is said. I did it. I did it with him, er . . . to him. They say he's dead. I don't remember. This doesn't mean there will be a debutante ball. I reserve my right to remain enigmatic by only injuring those who are already marginalized. I hurt with a look, maim with a touch, sever with a kiss, kill with a fuck. We had never done it. We could have. If we had, what would I be? Not homo; too narrow. Not hetero; only partly true. Not bi; too wishy-washy. My liaison would not have simply been with a man (men do not suit my tastes) but a suicidal insane black literate visionary impotent man. What prefix goes in front of -sexual to indicate a penchant for that kind of encounter? I won't be limited. I won't be marginalized. And if I have an encounter with a beautiful brunette woman who's perhaps a songwriter, a poet, a painter, or writer, someone with rough hands and child-bearing hips? What would you call me then? I will inoculate myself against your sophomoric categorizations the way cultures throughout history have defended themselves against demons of all sorts: through ritual. I will, at least once a year and as often as once per quarter spend an evening with an hermaphrodite. If s/he should have any other aberrant qualities, all the better: if s/he is a mulatto, or a dwarf, or an amputee, or is albino, or red-haired, color blind, deaf or mute, is feral or hirsute, is stricken with leprosy, or eats with his/her mouth open, or has any of a number of other qualities, a list of which I keep locked in my heart, I should be stricken. The more of these qualities in combination the better. We would meet only on equinoxes and solstices when the season is neither this nor that, and if the moon is new, better still, that we may be occulted. Thusly we would pass the hours, talking, touching, laughing, looking – upon emerging, it would be anyone's guess as to whether or not our intercourse had a sexual aspect or if it was a strictly social engagement. We would learn together to perfect the art of poker-face and to perform sleights of hand with tarot cards.

This will immunize me against your perverse habit of pinning people down. It's that habit of yours (sister) that killed Jesus. If you insist on uttering invectives, defining and limiting, I may allow you to consider me a litero-sexual. I am turned on by words, and the more open to interpretation the text is, the more erotic it becomes for me. The euphony of a foreign tongue is an aphrodisiac. Samuel Beckett was an eroticist of the first degree; James Joyce on the other hand, a mere pornographer. Should I mention the Bible? Ohh!

Later that day, Michael was found hanged to death in the showers. He was naked and had ejaculated at or near the moment of death. Because hanging victims often ejaculate as an involuntary reaction, no one, not even the coroner, could be certain if the death was a suicide, murder, or the accidental effect of an erotic practice. Just as Horace could have told them, Michael had left no note.

swan song

"You're the first man I've ever done it with."

"I will take responsibility for my actions, Sarah. But I tell you this now: I am an innocent man. I am completely without guile. I have neither preconceived notions nor ulterior motives. If necessary I can speak impeccable Mandarin Chinese without the slightest hint of an accent. I have no idea what I am doing here." Horace slid a hand across Sarah's silky thigh until he reached the hem of her skirt. He looked at her eyes.

She could smell her interest heightening as she looked up at the recessed lighting in what was her childhood home. Her father had passed just a few years after her mother had disappeared, undoubtedly with some gentleman (as her mother was fond of calling these other men in her life, some of whom were friends, some paying customers), to Bermuda or Tahiti, Portugal or Pago Pago or some other remote retreat where she could bask in luxurious surroundings, eating sumptuous meals ordered haughtily from black- or brown-skinned boys whom she never considered might have something on their minds more important than making certain that the bacon on her filet mignon was not twisted. Writhing on her barstool to put herself in a more accessible position, Sarah began humming a tune she had sung as a child with her mother. She closed her eyes and recalled the words.

> The sun always rises.
> It comes up in the East again,
> After the nighttime,
> Which after all is our friend.
> The sun will always come up again.
> Even when you think that the world is grey,
> Remember that tomorrow's another day.
> When things get bad and you want to run away,
> Remember what your mama say.

It was then that Sarah stopped humming.

"I feel absolutely Dutch."

"Get your fingers off of my cunt." The tears were streaming down her face. "I have to go paint. Please." She could think of nothing else.

The melody haunted him long after she left the room. He craved a consummate experience. Confused and frustrated, he threw a favorite book on the fire and simply watched it burn. As he curled into a fetal position, the tears welled in his eye and he wondered what Sarah was creating down there.

The basement was a great place to paint. She had been here for this purpose perhaps a thousand times before. Today it's gonna be different . . . somehow. Yes, finally, she thought, this is my home.

outward bound

Now that Sarah was expecting, Horace had to wonder what his next move would be. He felt at once both a sense of inevitability, of being pulled toward a predetermined destination, of helplessness in doing anything but following along with what fate had meted out for him, of bondage akin to the relationship one has with gravity, of irresistible attraction like authors often have toward making a moth-to-the-flame metaphor, of inescapability like a turd in a whirling vortex of toilet water or light into a black hole, and a sense of the enormous unending sequence of choices to be made, each one of which could stop or irrevocably alter one's life (for better or for worse).

This bifurcated sense of self, at once entrenched in two camps – power and powerlessness – reminded Horace of driving: those long treks of highway driving in which there is at once nothing to do but relax and enjoy the scenery and also the constant necessity of monitoring one's surroundings to be sure that Death does not come for her reward prematurely.

Highway driving always had a hypnotizing effect on him. He would use those hours to think up good life-experiences for himself on the basis that they might make interesting journal entries (and then plan how to carry them out), or would devote the travel time to meditation on an angel such as Metatron or contemplating how it was he might have slighted Anubis, confessing and reconfessing to himself memories stolen from a childhood not truly his own. Meanwhile, reentering conscious thought only as often as necessary, and by the end of the journey, he always felt as though the two or seven or thirteen hours he had spent in his vehicle had been transcended. He would make a circle of thought by tying one idea at the beginning of the trip to another at the end of the trip tied to a third idea from some other time in his life to establish it in a plane outside the trip and therefore disconnecting it from time, providing seven new thoughts unique to that journey which lay on the circumference of that circle.

Those seven new thoughts are irretrievable until one of them becomes the third idea defining the plane of thought in another journey, in which case six more become free to behave as they will with only chaos and entropy as their guides, in which case a driver in the oncoming lane attempts to pass with not enough room to spare, and Horace must now adjust by moving over onto the shoulder until the trouble should pass, and having come full circle he sees that no time has passed at all and even seven hundred miles is after all an illusory distance – still standing within the circle, the weight has simply shifted from left foot to right.

For a man to understand time is like a fish knowing in which ocean it swims.

revelations

I wish I had what it takes to be a homo . . . homosapien, homosexual, homoanything – as long as I'm around those who are like me; but alas, there are none like me. No one else thinks of life as a trip through the digestive tract of God, in which we are born the fruits of his labor, say apples. He eats us and then we are on a one way trip to Uranus, er . . . His anus. Any forestalling of death amounts to causing His constipation, certainly a sin worthy of its wage, while hastening our end, (that is, reaching His) prevents Him from standing. The King should seat himself neither too often nor too seldom. And we must strive to be not only apples, but all manner of comestibles, so that through our diversity, we may give Him consistency. Nothing enters through the end but ghosts and suppositories.

geneses

Journal entry/deathbed conversion/last will and testament:

I suppose I could have expected it. I walked through the door marked "entrance" fully expecting to be embraced by a world in which I would learn to be an unparalleled hypnotist, but instead found myself peerless and incommunicado vis-à-vis men, comrades, i.e., thou y usted et vous, etc. Despite the continuous flow of language (including words) not only did I not hold the power of suggestion over my fellow man, Horace said farcically, but I was for all intents and purposes invisible to the naked eye. It is only to the naked body that I come to light, and yet since nakedness and light happen to be both out of fashion at the moment I must at this point say goodnight, turn out the light, and try to remember why it was, so many moons ago, when I was mad, er . . . angry, that I wanted so urgently to get away from those who said they wanted only to help me. Master hypnotists can not be trusted. They only try to convince you that what is yours is theirs. When the enchantment is broken, Deus vobiscum – a loss of the sense of identity, Deus vult – a cessation of sexual arousal, Deus ex machina – your name is the only stimulus to which you respond.

reflections

I sat down again to write, and as I reached for my pen, I knocked a small mirror off of my table, which fell to the floor and broke into Sistine, er . . . sixteen pieces. With the shattering of that mirror, my inspiration to write was broken, and all that was left was a reflection. A reflection of the intended audience – a reflection of me – Sistine reflections – a nose here, an eye there, a mouth over there, and don't forget the ear. Reader, lend me your ear. Each fragment seemed to move and replace these body parts in almost random ways. If a Cubist had painted the Sistine Chapel, would a can of Campbell's soup have ever become an icon for the random assignment of value in art? The banal and ordinary events and objects in a well ordered world have taken on the role of unlikely masterpiece. My broken mirror on the floor is pure accidental genius; not my own genius, but the genius of God passing through me and manifesting itself as an accident. Now how can I get this off the floor and into a gallery without disturbing God's arrangement of these pieces where they all are now?

An X-ray technician knocks on my door as I am writing this and asks to take a picture of my hand. "It is busy," comes the reply. He says he will be back later for the photograph. Some primitive cultures who have had contact with industrialized peoples believe that a photograph traps the soul of the one pictured.

I believe I can get the aliens to move this mirror to a place where an audience will be able to access it. I continue to write. I feel it is not I who is writing, but a mysterious force writing through me. This is a close encounter of the literary kind. When I write, I become Xenos, the heretical Abyssinian.

I feel impervious. I want to walk across a bed of hot coals.
There are no coals, just fragments. I cross them . . . on foot.
I notice my feet are bloody, and the fragments of reflective are
no longer where God originally placed them, and I feel . . .
having bled, I feel . . . my thoughts are coming full circle . . .
the end of a cycle . . . I feel . . . the capacity to nurture.

Part III

. . . On Company Money

.

now and forever

I am having a stroke. A stroke of genius. I'm stroking my creative power center. I can see some genius just beginning to emerge from my creative power center. I'm having a stroke. A petit mal seizure, or more appropriately, a petit bene seizure. How many must die for one seed of creative genius to be planted in fertile soil to grow like a tree to be cut down, immortalized by serving as a canvas, upon which the Gutenberg Bible is printed. Or will it be here and then gone, ephemeral and transcendental, like an aborted foetus or a wad of toilet paper. Or will it straddle the line like Sarah straddles my creative power center. Right between here and there – The National Enquirer, People magazine, TV Guide – not quite toilet paper, not quite literature. Ugghh! I tear off a page of Hamlet and wipe up the mess I made while trying to prepare Sarah a drink.

factors of 0 and 1

I reach down into the cesspool that is human experience and pull up a golden nugget. I wipe off all the shit and try to polish it a little with my shirtsleeve in preparation of jotting it down, er . . . that is to say, throwing it back.

I am a computer. A stinking mainframe consecrated to the task of processing human waste products: words. Not word-processing, like simple type-cut-paste operations, but word PROCESSING, like sewage treatment. Taking the totality of words, which is univocal and monolithic, primordial and undifferentiated – in the beginning was the Word – and PROCESSING it, like the refining of sugar, sprinkling it over a bowl of shit and setting it before the waiting hoards of flies who will hungrily gobble it down (through no fault of their own . . . it is their nature to crave shit and sugar) and then, worst of all, they will talk about it, further intermixing it with the dead souls at the end of His digestive tract. The more we discuss a gathering of words, the further we sink into the mire of Philistinism.

Words of advice – always have a persona at your disposal. Treat words catholically. Eat mangoes. Read.

Try fucking your way to the top.

sound action

The almost effervescent modus operandi of several nearby

inconsequential submariners eventually eroded the faith of

almost every member of the Ugandan Nations' Assembly of Ass-

biters, due in part to the fact that all of those who had opted for

caffeine were writhing uncontrollably without the benefit of

certain compounds specifically formulated for the purpose of

attenuating the frequency of – and alleviating the discomfort

caused by the onset of – the untoward effects of parasitic

bacteria, er . . .

Several renegade Ugandan Marines poisoned the coffee of their U.N. delegates causing those who survived to fear for the stability of their political standing. (Meanwhile, back in the States) Horace experienced a moment of Dadaistic clairvoyance; a certainty stemming from the acknowledgement of the truth of the absurd; the revelation of the banal: a third world coup. Death by poisoning for the political representatives of a dissatisfied populace, whose homegrown assassins were now in the process of metamorphosing into representatives themselves. Another dusk. Another dawn. No such thing as Ugandan yogis. Nor Yogic politicians (until Thelema?) The sun will always come up again.

"Suck my thick black cock, you insane white manhole."

They say I busted his tooth. I wanted to vomit. Now a black

man lies dead in a heap on the floor, neck broken as if from

whiplash. A small pool of semen. Another of blood from the

corner of his mouth. Two teeth in his throat.

"What happened?"

"Unequivocally I can say he hung himself. He gave up his seat of power and thereby hung himself, metaphorically speaking, and thenceforth hung himself literally speaking. Where was my hand in this abominable tragedy? Far from the action, it was. Words create power; sound action.

"I had an idea. I wrote it down. Someone read it. A life expired. Is this a chronology? A causality? A phenomenon of synergy and synchrony, of imagined fellatio brought about by someone's implosive self-analysis, and the resultant serpentine shedding of the self-consuming demon Ego? I stared at the power center until I was blind . . . with rage . . . with desire . . . I sped down the avenue of hyperconscious thoughtlessness, one hand on the gear knob, Doppler downshifting into the third dimension until I could see nothing but the source, blackness, Dada. The skunk rolled down the hill and ruptured its larynx. And there was I . . . nearer to Thee, O Lord, yet silent. Approaching the zenith of a mountain of Nietzschean dimensions screaming inside my desire for attainment but outwardly as serene as Gautama and as silent as the cardiac thump thump of an unseen garter snake. Words create power . . . sound action.

medium rare

Each time I commit a character in writing, or rather a chain of characters bound to be seen as words and sentences, as meaningful representatives, each time a character is committed, each time a sentence is issued, each time a character is institutionalized in the nuthouse of words, that character loses something in terms of individuality. "A" in the word "anything" is no longer "A". It is now part of the system, incorporated into the greater context of "anything". Each time I commit a character in writing I do so with the honesty, the urgency, the candidness of a suicide. They always write exactly what's on their minds, never daring to speak it. They claim a power over the word and depart on that note. There is nothing more silent than a suicide who leaves no note.

In the beginning was the Word. The Word died. Nietzsche told us it is so. (See also McLuhan). "I am the Alpha and the Omega" – not a declarative, but rather an imperative. Made in his image, I must not only be committed to the Word, but must also be a character in my own right, else I shall be sucked into McLuhan's medium-sized brain. It is imperative to read Nietzsche. Then throw it away, Nietzsche is dead. Very dead.

All the pedants in Mumford stood up in unison and said in unison, "God is alive and well and He lives in the word."

When I read Nietzsche, all the letters jumped off the page and danced around on the paper. I once threw away a copy of "The Antichrist" because, and I swear, it had a picture of the Blessed Virgin made out of those letters dancing around on the page. (Why?)

Traditional Jewish mysticism teaches three mothers – Aleph,

Mem, Shin: another Holy Trinity. A trinity of virgins which, infused by Him, the Alpha and the Omega, resulted in, Christians believe, the Word made flesh.

McLuhan and Nietzsche announced the death of the Word. I am here to announce its triumphant return.

Step 1. Acknowledge and claim your death.

Step 2. Speak and write with frankness and honesty.

Step 3. Forsake the results (remember, you're going to be <u>dead</u>!)

Horace had a brief but significant out-of-body experience and realized

Step 4. When you rest, rest wordlessly.

bondage

The pen is mightier –
Words contain and confine.

Than the sword –
It cleaves from the piglets the swine.

Words contain
The secrets of harnessing

Time. Time and again the pen
Serves us – bacon and wine.

Horace wrote this poem on a napkin and gave it to Sarah. She wiped her eyes with it and put down her brush and palate and read the poem three or four times, then asked simply, "What does it mean?"

"It means I'm glad you're pregnant, I want the baby, and I was having a hard time finding the words to tell you. I'm gonna have a glass of wine. Do you . . . oh, um . . . I'm gonna have a glass of wine."

"Juice for me please."

"Mmhmmm."

They are silent as Horace pours drinks from a nearby shelftop refrigerator.

"I need to rest now."

A minute later, Horace says, "Mmhmmm," to an empty basement.

orbit

Horace finds himself in a spaceship piloted by (Jesus?) [Can't be sure; no halo, no parables, no feeling of being close to someone/something holy. Just a man with uncanny (solar) energy.] He explains that the red giants are emanations of His anger, which once they had been loosed, could not be recalled and reabsorbed until they had run their course as it were, unless he wanted to wage a jihad upon them, and it could be that between them all, they might figure it out that they had powers equal to His, albeit unused mostly, except for experiments in telekinesis and acts of charity. They were for all practical purposes physical manifestations of His mood, anger. And they would act according to the implications and circumstances of that mood. Angry at self – civil wars. Angry at others – space exploration, deep-sea diving. Angry at mother – pollution, forest fires. And when the anger subsides – the race is imperiled: wasting diseases, ozone depletion. Moments of repression are most dangerous – quakes, hurricanes, tornadoes, typhoons, tidal waves. Realization of the nature of anger – spontaneous combustions.

And when the anger subsides the race is imperiled?! What a dilemma! For their sake I must stay angry, no? Let my people go. What will happen to their souls? They will be like your anger, transformed . . . now let the dead bury the dead. And let the anger bury the anger – population explosion. Quiet now – we're entering orbit.

id

Writing is mental masturbation jerk

Penis

Continue genus

I'm a genius

Stroke my ego.

ZZZ... ZZZ... ZZZ... ZZZ... ZZZ... ZZZ... ZZZ... ZZZ... ZZZ... ZZZ... ZZZ... ZZZ... ZZZ... ZZZ... ZZZ...
...ZZZ...ZZZ...ZZZ...ZZZ...ZZZ...ZZZ...ZZZ...ZZZ...ZZZ...ZZZ...ZZZ...ZZZ...ZZZ...ZZZ...ZZZ...ZZZ...ZZZ

ZZZ...ZZZ...ZZZ...ZZZ...ZZZ...ZZZ...ZZZ...ZZZ...ZZZ...ZZZ...ZZZ...ZZZ...ZZZ...ZZZ...ZZZ...ZZZ...
ZZZ......ZZZ...ZZZ...ZZZ...ZZZ...ZZZ...ZZZ...ZZZ...ZZZ...ZZZ...ZZZ...ZZZ...ZZZ...ZZZ...ZZZ...ZZZ...

Sine off. No more sleeping. Wake to the writing. Go to bed writing. Dream writing. Drink writing coffee. Eat writing breakfast. Write writing. Wake up. Writing. Wake up . . . writing. Wake up.

quicksand

Fear – I am sinking further into the quicksand that is artistic thinking. Crazy people can relate to my words. My garbage disappears each time I put it in front of the place I live. Why do people take my garbage? And what do they do with it once they have taken it? I think they should not dump my garbage with the refuse of others, but should instead keep mine separate, stacked neatly and arranged symmetrically or enshrined and then burned at the new moon. Are only crazy people hired to take my garbage? I've thrown out lots of meaningful letters. At first I threw them out in anger but more recently in the spirit of house cleaning. One day I suppose I will find myself living in a sanctuary, er . . . asylum. A safe haven for cognitive slippers. A warm place to rest. Some quiet. A place I can learn to fly or to walk through walls, or to write about doing so. The Great Wall is 2000 miles long, but it's not 2000 miles high, and it's not 2000 miles thick. It can be seen clearly from space. My face turns really red when I am angry.

the moat

Before going any further with this tornado of metaphysical metaphor masquerading as a fictional flight of fancy, permit me to point out paradoxical and perplexing points about my persona, specifically Horace, son of O. Cyrus, a.k.a., etc., etc. First, English is not my native language, nor is it anyone's. Second, I like to write.

I like to write.

I'm not sure what the third is, but it has something to do with the voluntary and systematic dismantling of one's own psychic infrastructure towards a goal of discovering what it is that lay at the roots in order to build up from that foundation, rather than creating castles in the air.

Further notions of a mad(?)man: at the root of speech is silence. At the root of writing is psychic imprinting. The two processes, speech and writing, are not as is commonly believed predicated one upon the other, but rather are as independent from and unrelated to each other as smoke signals and tattoos.

Therefore, the natural conclusion to be drawn from these hypotheses is this: speech gets us nowhere. It folds back in upon itself eventually falling silent. Although in the short term it may generate more speech, it always comes to naught, enveloped by that which bore I unto the air, much like the universe itself which expands to fill the infinite then collapses upon itself unable to resist the gentle insistence of the void. Whereas writing on the other hand comes from the primeval, the collective, and its results are permanent, visible and evocative. It is not bound by acts of commission to feelings of guilt, but rather is obligated by ancestry not to omit, for the results of omission are well (un)documented: wars, alien abductions, poltergeists and other risen undead. To stop writing history is to allow history to write itself. To stop writing fiction is to allow fiction to write itself. To stop writing philosophy is perhaps a good idea.

Dearest reader, if you intend to write, listen carefully to what your character says; s/he will tell you how s/he is to be written, and if you visit a tattoo parlor before the work is complete, you'd bloody well better not speak to the artist.

Jeffrey,

Due to the unique nature of your piece, I could up until this point, overlook your unwillingness to stick with either the first or third person viewpoint, but here you break with the rules you've set up for yourself as a framework and in the process, I believe, completely lose the average reader with respect to which p.o.v. s/he should identify with (sic). First was Horace speaking in the first person, second was the narrator speaking in the third person, but now there is a third, speaking in first person who is not Horace, for Horace always indents his speeches, and not our narrator, who always speaks in third person. But rather this new player seems to have supplanted our invisible narrator the way a channeled spirit displaces a medium. Eureka! Did we not also see this player during the interrogation of the patient in chapter 15? Who is this new "I"? From where did s/he come? What is the purpose of bringing in a new unexplained viewpoint especially at this relatively late stage of the story? I believe the problems unveiled in this chapter are indicative of those of the entire piece, and I suggest you begin a rewrite immediately with an eye toward creating one unified point of view, else you may kiss this project *auf wiedersehen*.

Your editor,

Adolph Fienstaine

Dear Editor,

You
are
fired.

Sincerely

The three of us

a koan

Horace's mind was beginning to rest and his body was soon to follow when he found himself telling his healer, his confessor, his confidant, his projected sympathetic other, his mind reader, just what all his effort was aimed at . . . release. Release from the institution. Release from madness. He wanted to stop being mad. Instead he fell asleep and began a grotesque dream. In this dream, he had fallen asleep in a traditional Japanese home, his own to be sure, for he was sleeping a traditional Japanese sleep, dreaming a traditional Japanese dream, wearing a silk kimono (also presumably traditional Japanese).

In this mad sleep, the sleeping man who was a foreigner to his natural self was being haunted by the image of one thousand and one single-eyed Daruma dolls, a new one having appeared each night for nearly three years. A thousand and one hopes dashed – each but a fantastickal flight of fancy. Nearly three years this Japanese man had spent inside this house of translucent barriers and a view of the unmoving master Fuji-san, each night drawing in the one eye, retreating into meditation upon the problem – how to leave this house – but waking up each morning unable to draw in the other: wish unfulfilled. He found himself only wanting to gouge out his eyes, frustrated at having had the wish at all. Alien nightmare ends.

Mad dreams come to rest.

Doctor explains the traditional symbolism of Zen master Daruma dolls. Make wish, draw in one eye. Wish fulfilled, draw in other eye. Also Daruma doll egg-shaped – often fall down, always stand back up. But Horace not egg-shaped. Also Horace always have both eyes, but still in madhouse. Maybe Daruma self-blinding yogi . . . maybe Horace not understand concept of vision.

horticulture

Is it magic? I imagine what it's like when you open your legs. Is it magic? Giving birth to new ideas.

Is it magic? I imagine what it's like when you open your mouth. Is it magic when it comes? . . . the word? In the beginning, that's all there was. You there with your legs open giving birth; multiply exponentially, ad infinitum. You with your jaw dropped accepting life-giving seed . . . the word. Over and over, I give you the thrust of my message, of my power, and I can only hope that one day you will accept it. But now there is no longer only me. No longer only you and I, but something greater now comes between us, between you, among us, within you. And now the seed, the word, the beginning is no longer just lovingly devoured, but instead is lovingly invested in the child – the one who was not and is and shall be (eating mangoes).

What have you created in that basement of yours – that foundation-mind of yours? Will I know the child? Will the child know me?

Dear reader, pray not for me, but will nature take its course. It is better you did so than spend an eternity searching for that which may or may not exist. Selah.

the end

It is here in the madhouse that words find their end. Mishima committed seppuku over and over again in word before finally being committed in deed. Miller used this place as his personal confessional until there was nothing left to confess but "I am". Should I mention Crowley? Ohh! The world needs fewer martyrs.

The secret to working in a church is to mind your p's and q's. Other letters are as important, but it is the dictates of social decorum that keeps madmen voluntarily mute.

When Jesus opened his mouth in utterance, he did not so much speak as he did write on the souls of men. This was not exactly polite, and he died for it. Would the world have been a much different place if he had simply gotten off the mothership and silently observed for thirty years? Or was he, by being born, a sheep who had strayed from the flock and who had to bleat in order to find his way back to (death's) flock? Is it death which interrupts the flow of life? Our vanity tells us it is so. But is it not equally as valid to say that it is life which interrupts the constancy of that which is both before and after life?

Who dares interrupt my death?

free fall

Horace's thoughts were racing madly as he lay on top of Sarah and so he decided his coitus needed some interruptus. He muttered some pretend concerns about aliens until Sarah rolled him off of her and complained about the difficulty of becoming impregnated (although she already had become so).

Horace at last had come to an understanding about what was attractive about being human. It was the guiltlessness with which people came out and mixed with their own kind (and in a microcosmic parallel, the homosexual community of homosapiens did likewise). He no longer felt a curiosity to become one and resolved to be the best alien, er. . . heterosapien he could. He remounted his human wife and redoubled his efforts at creating a halfbreed child, from her flesh and his word.

Children are created, that is to say conceived, immaculately. That is to say, they are conceived in a pure state, so rare among humans. That state is one of bliss, of ecstasy. The closest thing most humans know to religious rapture is the orgasm, and it is of that moment that humans are conceived. During that moment we are lost in the moment, we exist only in the moment and only for the moment. Horace was no different in that respect.

the castle grounds

I have journeyed a long time trying to reach this world. They call it Earth and they call themselves human. I call it disillusionment and I've reached it. I am an alien here – no illusions. Once I had spoken. I had said, "No illusions." But what was heard was delusions, er . . . "delusions".

I am not homo; about that I have no illusions. I am not mad; there is no reason. I am not a yogi; the sun still hurts my eyes. Mangoes are a tropical fruit. Dragonflies are bugs; telepathy has not been empirically substantiated. I'm going to be a father. The church pays poor wages, especially for well-constructed sin. Nostradamus was a poet. What goes up must come down (excepting quantum physics). Finding religion means a vast leap of faith. Ezekiel visited the twentieth century via astral travel. Cars are a necessary evil until mankind sprouts wings. Heaven is far away. But not as far as you may think. My release date has been set. The sun will eventually burn out. My vision is not what it used to be. I'm going to be a father.

her majesty's chariot awaits

Having been ejected from his home by the One he loved, Horace had retreated to a gentleman's club, although he did not feel much like a gentleman as he observed the human female "Boom-Boom" Barbie on the elevated runway. She was involved busily in the removal of occludents from her soul carriage. It was questionable just how much soul remained in her carriage. The line of work in which she was engaged tended to take these women's humanity, their tenderness, their charm and receptivity, their grace and sensuality, and their sensitivity, and replace them with mechanical simulacra of the same. That, Horace thought, is what makes a place like this obscene. The fact that the icon of the human female is sacred here makes it tolerable.

Just then Horace began coughing a hacking cough. It was relentless. In a place such as this, men don't notice what other men are doing. There was no one to help Horace as he underwent what amounted to be a life-threatening, although relatively quiet ordeal.

Men who frequent nightclubs like these often smoke and drink heavily. A man with a cough was no extraordinary sight here. Horace did most of the coughing into his fists and tried to keep eye contact with the dancers – to show nothing was wrong – so as not to cause a scene – and help keep egos afloat.

"Boom-Boom" watched momentarily from between her knees the upside-down image of Horace alternately throat-clearing and coughing. He seemed almost polite about it. A rare thing around here, politeness. He coughed small and into his hands. Horace admired Barbie's assets but was too busily engaged in dislodging this foreign substance from deep within him to display his admiration in the way to which she was accustomed.

This thing Horace was expectorating [and you, dear reader, perhaps have been expecting] had been lodged since childhood in a place one might rationally imagine to be the bile duct; and he was finally getting rid of it.

invitation

I have an inner eye with which to see, inner ears with which to hear. There's ringing in my ears. The sound of bells. A wake up call. Striking a balance. Libra, libre, let freedom ring. Church bells, wedding bells, ceremonial gong. Is she gone? While I was standing at the altar staring into the very heart of the sun, did she walk away? Or did she slither off? Or perhaps she disappeared under the veil of a cloud of smoke and a blinding flash of light.

She is Kali, the divine Mother. (Like a bug) she has six limbs. She has four arms – two with which she raises her kinder, two with which she beheads the mischievous.

I hear the beating of the ceremonial drum, like peals of thunder and I know that our task has begun. A commingling and conjoining, an intermixing and intertwining. In short, (distant sonic rumbling) marriage. It takes two to tango. Sarah, would you care to dance? Sarah?

Part IV
...In The Abyss

Since arriving here, I've been watching my death in the same way that others watch TV. They never shut it off. TV is my life in here. It is a common misconception that the sun gives life to all who are touched by its rays, but that is TV's role . . . the fact is that we are born immortal and the sun drains away that life force, efficiently, ruthlessly. Hence Lucifer, the light-bringer's bad reputation. I am practicing averting my eyes from the TV, only looking at it indirectly; projected through a pinhole for instance. While coincidentally I am considering how I might be able to watch the sun more closely without adverse effects.

Now there is a nature show on the ward's G-wing video screen. I can hear the playful voice-over from my chair facing the window. "Od's bodkins! It's the devil's darning needle dancing his delicate rhumba in mid-flight. This curious insect, more commonly known as the dragonfly, while completely harmless to humans, is an extremely accurate and lethal hunter, honing in like a hawk on his next source of sustenance by what seems to be something akin to psychic powers."

Later in the same program a hawk is shown having his eyes seeled. "It's part of his training regimen. When the stitches are taken out, he'll no longer need to rely on his eyesight to find what he's after."

Someone changed the channel by remote control. No one seemed to notice the difference. Exotic music is playing. A deep and deliberate voice carefully booms out, "The eye of Horus has been associated (even down to today) with inner sight and protection from evil. Take for instance this modern mystery writer who carries the eye with him through each page of the writing process. 'It helps me scrutinize my writing with an eye toward eliminating anything at all that does not significantly add to the story, because as any writer knows, what doesn't help your story hurts it. Now really as Egyptian legend has it, Thoth rules over writing itself, so I often consult the book of Thoth, or the tarot as it's more commonly called, for ideas which true to form for Thoth usually end up being about or having resonance with the idea of justice, for which the mystery genre is well suited. And I find that writing with a white quill pen helps me tune into Thoth's energy very immediately and powerfully. But anyway, Horus also has a resonance with justice, not like a judge on the bench as Thoth does, but avenging a wrong, and with his protection from evil resonance he's great for editing, and the inner sight which is so closely connected with the icon of the eye of Horus has always been invaluable to me in finding holes, even minuscule ones in my stories, because anything that is left undone in a story that someone has spent several hours of his or her life reading is just maddening. Plot holes and gaps in character development, underdeveloped subplots, indecipherable chronologies, the introduction of characters and/or events without backstory and/or follow through; these things just drive readers <u>NUTS</u>! People become mad after realizing that something they've spent a recognizable portion of their life doing is meaningless. And that's really where Horus (the hawk-headed god) and the eye of Horus come into play. At least for me. Now you may have an altogether different experience of Horus depending on your certain circumstances, but there's always an element of wrongs righted wherever Horus is evident. Often times the righting takes a different form than the wronging did, but there's still an evening out, a sense of chaos dispersed and order restored, which is such a bedrock of the entire Egyptian cosmogony.' The

Pyramids at Giza. The Sphinx . . . The hows and whys of these larger than life monuments raise larger than life questions for Egyptologists and laymen alike. Was it years of backbreaking labor for hundreds of thousands of men that put these structures in place? Some ancient technology unknown to modern man whose secrets lay encrypted on the walls of an undiscovered passageway in one of those very tombs? Or were these monolithic mysteries placed here as some believe by an extraterrestrial intelligence?"

"Aaaaaaaaaaaaggggghhhhh!"
"Aaaaaaaaaaaaggggghhhhh!"
"Rrrreeeeeeeeyaaaaaahhhh!
"Ooohooohooohooohooohoohoohoohwhahaahaahahhaieeyah!"
The screams on the G-ward became numerous and loud. It was apparent that the mad were not happy. And then something unusual happened. Someone found the power switch - and used it.

Horace was compelled to put down his pen, which he had just been using to write the following diary entry:

Sarah, oh crowned jewel of my space-age elastic polymer imagination, did you ever notice the human ability to become entranced upon entrance? The homonymy of the two words begins with English, that is, they have completely different origins, but like Romeo and Juliet they are drawn together and together they will come to their respective (or mutual if you prefer) ends. It happens in love. We enter into affairs of the heart (and mind and body and soul) and become impenetrable to other forces; the advice of friends, common sense, logic, monetary concerns – although years later we may look back in astonishment and wonder, "Was I nuts? What was I thinking carrying on with that person?" This entrancement also happens with life itself. During the first two or three years, we are not so immersed in the rhythm of life as to be exclusively in life. At that age we still have one foot in the Protoplasm: conscious of something other than what is occurring in this trance-like state known as life. This is why we cannot remember the beginnings of life, and coincidentally why the elderly have what we who are further from the edges of life's timeline refer to as senile dementia, which is really nothing more remarkable than the obverse side of childhood precocity, the latter being an accelerated turning toward life, and the former away. When I entered this place I thought there was no way out. I wanted to find a way to stay forever. I planned my escape. I developed my ideas for a better Mumford. Eventually I admitted to myself that I was here and I was here for a reason and I had walked in on two feet; I had not materialized here from a transporter aboard a mother-ship (although the analogy is rather nice) and that I would be here for a long time – however long – it was then that I began to wake up from my long sleep (I had to jot down my dreams to keep from forgetting them.) An alien consciousness overtook me. I was imbued with a sense of the divine. I forgot how to ride a bicycle. My inner eye found focus and honed in on the central core of my existence. Some of what I found there, I cannot use words to describe, some has been written in the pages of this book. Some I can not remember. How long have I been here? When I return to the outside, how will I find you? I will come to the marketplace on the day of the spring equinox following my release. You will recognize me by my penchant for ripe mangoes. I will be the bookish-looking one; the one focusing Zen-like on that spot in his mind where the anger once had been. I will be choosing ripe mangoes for a nourishing meal, and there may be an empty tin of sardines at my feet. You will find me. There are certain things and there are words. I can't go on. I must go on.

The ward had fallen silent.

Following, an excerpt from the pages of Horace's diary from the period known as the lost years. This period was the one in which he progressed greatly in his ability to reflect upon his thoughts accurately in verbal form, becoming quite warm and candid although his tendency toward literalism occasionally came to the fore. Notice the lack of double entendres, ambiguities, metaphors, hyperbolic analogies, and other elusions (sic) of grandeur.

[...]

The doctors wanted Sarah to go under the knife for exploratory surgery. They weren't certain what the problem was, but she wasn't communicating. Actually, they weren't certain there was a problem other than persistent stubbornness, but she had been milling about the hospital for some time now and had not offered a single word. When the powers that be asked her about surgery, she said nothing in the way of dissent and then remained passive as she was prepared for surgery, so most concerned were convinced they were prepared to operate on a consenting subject. They did not and could not know the extent of her consent; just how willing she was or wasn't to be explored and poked and prodded and probed in a crude attempt, scientifically speaking, to determine the nature of her refusal to communicate anything at all of any significance. It was not as though she had become catatonic though, she just would not speak. And beyond that, she had found a way to carry herself such that her body language and face were also expressive of nothing. She was a tabula rasa, a pool of water, still and pure, reflecting back upon the reader, er . . . looker, what he or she saw there. She was a glass eye, a crystal ball, saint and sinner, priest and whore, doctor and patient, the understanding and the bewildered, the sun and the sun eclipsed, the visionary and the blind, the deaf and the deafening, the major and the minor, mango and seed, lip and hood, man and wife and beast and burden, the virus and its cure, hermit and consortium. She had become both the main point and the digression.

I just experienced a phantom sensation in my missing foreskin, a phantom development in my missing character, a phantom incident in my missing plot, some phantom guilt from my missing mother, a phantom moment of telepathy with my missing wife, a phantom sense of relevance in relation to my missing historical perspective, a phantom fan letter from my missing readership, and a phantom reason for my missing journal pages.

Why do I keep a journal like this? Is it because I want to be able to look back on these words and say, "Look how mad I was!"? Is it because I want to be able to look back on these words later and say to another, "Look how angry I was!"? Is it because I want others to look upon these words saying, "Look how hard he worked to avoid leaving phantoms!"?

I look forward anxiously toward Halloween when I can reconnect with these phantoms of mine.

"Sarah . . . wake up. Sarah? Wake up, Sarah. Sarah?"

Sarah slowly parted her anaesthesia-induced, narcotic-augmented, sleep-encrusted eyes and dryly croaked a feeble "Hi" to husband and father-to-be Horace.

"How long was I out?"

"Shhhh. That's not important."

"Horace, come closer."

He did.

"I had a dream. I was a nymph: a wood nymph, dancing and floating through the air in the deep recesses of a forest glen . . . a favorite of your youth. My hair was red like fire and you were absent from my mind completely, as if dead. As I began to let my mind wander to thoughts of love and what my ideal lover might be like, I realized I was lost. The trees began speaking to me telling me which way to go. At first I ignored these voices from the woods, after all, they were trees. But what they were telling me made sense. I cannot remember what it was they said because it was not in words as such and yet the ideas came across clearly nonetheless. I remember thinking as I was being bombarded with ideas generated from the forest by the trees, each thought louder than its predecessor, often overlapping and/or contradicting the others, 'This is insanity.' Madness is a tool used by the mind to counteract information overload."

Sarah had now been whispering this anecdote to Horace for over fifteen minutes, and her throat was now very hoarse.

"So how do you account for the existence of insanity prior to the post-modern condition?" Sarah whispered inaudibly.

Horace leaned in toward her until his ear nearly touched her lips.

"Time travel."

I would like at this point, late 'tho' 'tis, to make a leap from

this precipice of faith toward the end, er . . . (possible)

conclusion of this diarrhea've mine, er . . . journalistic rampage,

toward assimilation, concretion, a compounding of me

(and me)

and my mad, and maddening

(I'll say)

attempts at expression, and

(self-expression)

by way of this metaphorical leap-frogging find myself

(in a manner of speaking)

less mad than before and more able to navigate these dreams,

these footpaths, these business trips and these lives.

(perhaps fictional)

Those around me to whom I had formerly clung

(mad thought)

are now gone. It won't be long, on a geological scale, before I

too am one of those who has passed from pre-existence to
apparent to appearance to . . .

(apotheosis)

disappearance, and reemergence as preeminent
transcendentalist/fictionalist/journalist/travel essayist . . .
or is all this a simple matter of . . .

(delusions of grandeur)

finding my way, as if trailblazing, to continue to write, 'tho' 'tis
toward a destination unknown that I dream-walk-travel-plunge.
Family and friends now gone, I must write myself

(right myself)

new ones.
    Hence Sarah and the child and the increasing frequency of
blank journal pages.

    I had succeeded in confounding my journal-peekers' temporal
sense, and so the healers wanted to confabulate with me but
did not want me to confabulate for them. They were grown
weary of fiction.

THE END IS NEAR.

To indent or not to indent is no longer the question. During a latter confabulation between the staff and Horace, he relayed this tale, presumably of a dream:

"One of us did battle last night with an eel, fifty feet in length, in a swimming pool of brackish water. An onlooker, after the deed was done, commented anticlimactically and somewhat enigmatically, that the fighter who had not been engaged was 'even clunkier'."

The eel is a formidable foe but is metaphorically no match for the dragonfly.

"When the battle was over I noticed someone sitting lotus-style at the edge of the pool, serene. His hands formed the so-called contemplation mudra, his chin was tucked in, his breathing was soft and deep and his ample penis hung quite naturally. He was unconcerned about, though fully aware of the conflict taking place. He generated among those around him thoughts of wife and child and a sort of consensual intuition regarding the absurdity of a notion such as alien observation."

"Horace, please stick to the facts."

"What do Oedipus Rex and Daruma have in common?"

(The family that plays together stays together.)

"The eel is dead." (Long live the eel.)

(The family is like a simile.)

Letters are related to each other in word families, paragraph clans, chapter tribes, accumulated-meaning peoples.

"Doctor, how do you keep your family together?"

"I think we're getting a little ahead of ourselves, don't you Horace?"

The success of Sarah's recent operation had still not been determined as of the handing down of this sentence.

The methuselah's thanatos . . . The old man had died. The madness eventually dissipated, that is to say, while it did still exist, it no longer found a way to express itself. So many blank pages. Other pages filled with the term tabula rasa over and over again, like a written invocation – R.S.V.P. . . Dear God or gods, your presence is requested to honor the joining of ideas and words for the eventual purpose of creating more words precipitating further ideas, etc., etc., reception to follow, God or gods willing. And step and . . . the end is near . . . choke . . . qoph . . . involuntary man's laughter. Laughter came easily to Horace now that he was no longer mad, yet the deaths of his father and friend were no laughing matters. It was the eel that brought this about, thought Horace. Then he thought, "My thinking is clearest when angry or wooing, least clear when enraged or in love, but I am most clear when not thinking," and at that, resolved to stop fanning the flames, although he couldn't resist wishing for a stiff breeze from time to time, after all, cold turkey, though traditional after Thanksgiving, did not have the Zen appeal of broiling eel. Deep in meditation sometime shortly prior to his release, Horace imagined his self, his sitting self; the one in meditation, transforming into a red giant, there on the floor, expanding and contracting, breathing, focusing on one point, near Sirius the dog star, full of madness, trying to return, to become Earthbound. Across time he was hearing the vague mutterings of one who might someday be his fiancée, perhaps then his wife. She was beckoning him, he imagined, from across time, across a crowded room. Was she communicating to him, or was he putting words in her mouth the way the muse put words in him? The doctors would not say. They couldn't tell. Regulations. They swore. A healthy sign of anger. It wasn't blood she wanted. Not sangre, but rather sangria.

>She wanted to drink not my blood, but my soul, and such a
>cocktail, poured voluntarily was not so much poison but
>panacea to all who were similarly disposed to him doing the
>pouring, and so what could I do but determine to pilot my craft
>to her, come hell or high water (both did). Fueled by ideas and
>driven for a period by solitude to dash like a comma, er . . .
>comet, my journey was punctuated by hope and grief, despair
>and faith, joy and anger, until inevitably I landed my craft safely
>though not as quietly as I would have liked, looking at it now in
>retrospect. I exited the ship from beneath the stern in a move
>which may have been misinterpreted as a Trojan horse. I
>announced my arrival to a gaping and mystified throng.
>Intending to incite the crowd to gather under my protective
>wing, I urged them to, "Do as I say and no one will get hurt,"

also misinterpreted. Their group-will produced a blue-suited
man who adorned me with odd jewelry and brought me here to
be with others like me. Ones who had traveled far, much farther
than their natural years would allow. Ones who crave mangoes
and eel and concern themselves with the digestion of the gods.
There are none like me. I know this to be true. I am not mad. I
am not mad.

Now the problem had been named: how to get beyond these near-death experiences, these
close encounters, this madness, these words, this book, this alter-ego, these literary
references, these half-baked philosophies, these alliterations, this sophomoric free-verse
poetry, these feelings of distrust in this universe of my construction and get on with the
business of bringing the child into this world – that is to say reconciling misanthropy with the
understanding that I am, er . . . Horace is all too human, neither more nor less exceptional
than any other.

I had clung to my cynicism, my nihilism, for so long because
they had become a comfort to me in the face of all that had
come before, yet to dislike humanity and at the same time feel
human, at times too human, is the proverbial house divided.
Being human was an alien concept to me. I didn't know how to
behave. I thought at any time I might be discovered as an
imposter, and yet I was human, right? Two legs? Check. Two
arms? Check. Two nostrils, two ears and a mouth? Check. But
also two eyes. Eyes that have seen the suffering of humankind
unfolding like the pages of a book. (Eyes now blind.) A book is
interactive – while you read it, you may also be writing it as
well. The Bible is a fine example. This diary is not so fine. You
are all masons, laying the bricks in which I will be entombed.
You are all philistines. You are crucifiers. Ancient Egyptians

believed that thinking occurred in the heart or ab. Can't we please leave it there?

How do I get out of this infinite loop, this perpetual motion, this orbit, this womb, this karmic wheel? Mummy? Wake up. You're asleep. You're having a dream. Your eyes, dear reader, are moving and you are asleep, therefore you must be dreaming. Of what are you dreaming? Some crazy writer who thinks he is an alien? Some alien with a travel journal who thinks he's extraordinary? Or is there some vague resonance, some deeper something, recognizable though vague, in this business of sleepwalking, for which I am ostensibly your guide?

*   *   *

This is the first time I have picked up the pen in over two months. As part of the ritual to invoke the God or gods, I had sacrificed my writings, pen and all, to the demigods, who incidentally kept me in the prayer hall full time over the last eleven and one half weeks. In fact, I am at the altar even now as I write this, my first entry since way back when. What have I been doing with my time?

(Sic)

I've been developing some

(Bullshit)

philosophy (sic) and watching lots of TV. Actually the one arose out of the other. Many of the patients here had been complaining to the nurse on the ward about the incessant invasion of TV signals into our lives, always planting these seeds . . . trying to make candy and violence and sex without nudity take root in our lives until someone suggested we tape our own programming right here on the grounds of the asylum. I was given a camera and told to tape anything which interested me and so I turned it on and did not stop taping until the cassette ended. I rewound the tape and spent the next hour reliving the previous hour by watching everything that had just happened to me again, although this time instead of seeing everything through my eyes, I was seeing everything through-my-eyes-once-removed. But isn't that what dying is for? Upon realizing this, my life flashed before my eyes. I began to replay in my mind's eye the moment I had come to the realization. TV as substitute death was yet another egomaniacal assertion of the type that got my pens taken from me in the first place. I was supposed to be making journal entries toward the goal of removing the madness; the anger at the root of this madness, yet here I was conjecturing as to the significance of television's retrospective capabilities and wondering why 98% of American households own a set, why there's always one on in the ward, why comedies and death are such common programming and what it would take to get people to create their own programming on a massive scale. At least that way people would be watching their own deaths and not the laughably simulated death of some laughably simulated person who had only been alive for half an hour or half an hour at a time (or ostensibly so).

Please God or gods, take these pens away, give me laughably simulated closure, remove the madness, let nature take its course, give Michael iron will (that none may be unjustly injured by these lunatic rants), may my unborn child be a source of strength and wisdom to others and may I be a source of comfort to my phantom fiancée. May the fallacy of time's linearity be straightened out and this madness be dispelled. Lord Buddha be compelled. Anger be felled. If the ink would stop flowing I could quit looking for places on this soul carriage to visit with this, my angry pen.

"Boom-Boom" Barbie was tattooed from head to toe. She had an eel around her genitals beginning with its head just above her pudendum continuing down one thigh, between the lower vulva and rectal opening, back up her other thigh, and the tail was inside its mouth. Horace could not dally with her. Solipsism strictly forbidden. She had tried to cover it with a dragonfly and then a red herring.

I loathe the way wordsmithing demands precision. It's more
akin to surgery than painting.

Sarah was recovering nicely. In her basement was a still life, but what she embodied had
movement.

The child was the reason for Horace's madness, the child inside him, the child growing
inside her. The child on paper. It was the child which haunted his dreams. It was the child
which required his attention – when he wrote, when he didn't write, when he slept, when he
walked, when he swept the church aisle where his bride to be would be whenever that would
be. When he sat in meditation, it was the child would dilute his concentration. When he swam,
it was the child would keep him afloat. When he approached the castle, it was the child would
become the moat. The child was full of alligators and electric eels. It was spring fed and
dragonflies hovered over it constantly. It had a crown of thorns, it had a pair of horns, it was a
caricature. It made history at every turn. It was irritable. It was sexual. It was innocent and
disarming. It was engaging and it had a way of getting under your skin. It was constantly
hungry but never complaining. It was an egomaniac and yet purely id. Idiotic and idiomatic,
idiosyncratic and partially blind. It had a mind of its own. It was in the zone. It was love full-
blown. Red giants obeyed its will. It was one of them yet beyond them. It was superior. Words
to describe it are inferior. In fury are the aliens who come for it and find less than it. A stack of
letters in its place; love letters yes, but virtually meaningless nonetheless. The child is a labor
of love, sent from above to relieve the madness. Lift the sadness. Kiss the bride. What a ride.

The inside of an alien vessel is like a cocoon, like a womb.
One breathes an amniotic-like fluid; it is nourishment. It is rife
with language and like the cosmos, sparsely substantive. Mostly
a vacant environment with a little speck of potentially life
sustaining material here and there like specks of pepper in a
bowl of primordial soup. No intoxicants, no cigarettes, no way
out except to wait or abort or expire prior to deboarding. I must

keep in mind how long it takes to carry a child to full term. I've been writing about the child, trying to coax it out, watching its development here in the alien vessel, continually counting the number of digits, praying for a safe landing and normal adjustment to terrestrial existence. Ground control says signs are good. I guess that's a judgement call we each have to make. Ground control deals only in signs. Little electronic bleeps on a radar screen. Radio detecting and ranging. Change the station. Take control. Amniocentesis indicates snafu. Something on the screen we haven't seen before. We don't recognize it as one of our own. It looks like the other blips on the screen, but the motions it is making are not like ours. I think that was the child kicking; trying to kick its way out of this vessel. Pushing the envelope. Off of the screen. That's better. Nothing obstructing the view anymore. The tower is giving clearance. The final chapter of my book (which, by the way, is quite adaptable to movie form) is about to begin. I call it "Take Me To Your Leader" and they respond with a coded message in which a number appears enclosed in a circle, a hand sweeps around the circle in increments of a twenty fourth of a second and at the end of each cycle the number changes from 10 9 8 7 6 5 4 3 until 2 at which time, "blip" and the numbers disappear and the story begins.

The story begins with the disappearance of a blip and the emergence of fiction. The end of the creation of a book and a means to that end are here in the diary. Why are we here? To see the end. The Mayans say the end will come in 2012, after the death. I cannot keep ascribing and describing the madness, scribbling and conscripting these words for another fifteen years. This manuscript circumscribes the anger. It is the ritual of scarification. It is secretly concerned with criticizing the superscribes. It is diacritical, establishing a criterion for discerning hypocrisy. It's about sifting the wheat from the chaff, seed from the shaft, a leather quiver for arrows, cupidity, word roots. It's about growing up and letting go. Cutting the umbilical cord and transcribing one's dreams, one's nightmares, one's dark horse, one's ship that comes in, hitting the jackpot, knavepot, princepot or whatnot. It's about knowing when the canvas has been covered with ink, when the picture has been painted, when one's life has become still. A distillation of what has come before. An understanding of a chronology. The intoxication that comes with the recognition of the twisted circularity of a most august Möbius and the stripper named Barbie. The abyss opens up into a dream. Ghosts and suppositories are the stuff of nightmares. A poor sense of direction and one may find oneself asking, "Was this place always here?" and feeling at the end of one's rope, and dreams, strange dreams are the stuff books are made of.

In the madhouse where the television was always on, there was a news flash about a child called I . . . perhaps a foreshortening of something greater, having fallen into a well, a private hell, an abyss built by masons, filled with the stuff of life. Words can not do justice to the Herculean, er . . . Protean efforts being made to extract the child. Scolding and coaxing didn't do the trick. Lowering the rope seemed only to make matters worse. Reading Beckett soothed him a little, as did the occasional introduction of sexual stimulation, although even this was diminishing in its efficacy. There was to be only one way out of this womb-tomb: up. Beyond the ecosphere, the amniotic fluid, above the words, transcending ego, breaking out of orbit, cutting the tether to the mothership, sobering the drunken monkey, chanting "AUM" and meaning it, resting wordlessly, coming to terms with the eel, dodging the dragonfly, marrying the toad, landing the craft, confiding the dreams, whispering into the ear, swimming the moat, learning tattoo, killing Nietzsche and eating mangoes. I would climb his way to the mouth of the abyss on a mountain of the pits of the mangoes from which he had fed, and then he would give up mangoes forever, I thought. I was tired.

"Well, well, well, Horace. Now that you've left the hospital, are you ready for release? Now that the ceremony has been performed, are you ready to consummate? Before you lay with me, are you prepared to ravish the whore inside? I was at the gallery today and a book publisher asked me about your diaries. I have no idea how he heard about them in the first place, but I'm guessing he may have been at Mumford around the same time you were. He kept saying, 'I'd have to be crazy to want to publish those diaries, but I do.'"

"Did he call himself Doctor?"

"He said he could save your skin."

"I thought Boom-Boom would do that."

"Who's Boom-Boom?"

"Oh that's what I call the alien phenomenon."

Are you talking about abductions or just the fly-bys? Or maybe you mean walk-ins."

"Walk-ins?"

"Soul displacement."

"Eureka! Kind of like being born again?"

"Catholically speaking, yes."

"And technically?"

"Well, it ain't reincarnation."

"But these days, what is?"

"Took the words right out of my mouth."

"How was he gonna do it?"

"Save your skin you mean."

"Yeah, that's it."

"By tattooing you, soaking you in sour cream sauce and publishing your book, he would save your skin."

"Was he serious?"

"He was kind of laughing when he said it, so it was hard to tell."

"It is hard to tell. It's always hard for them. They're experts at not knowing how to tell. Experts at not knowing."

"Not hard for them to tell. Hard for me."

"It is."

"Hard to tell."

"I'm not the man I used to be."

"Why don't you insert the videotape. Maybe that'll get things going."

Well, I feel like I may never get out of here. I may never want to. Some things are cathartic. Pornography, Joyce, Nietzsche, the diaries . . . I'm not so sure it's good for me to publish the diaries."

"Yeah, but porno's not supposed to be good for you either. Now get over here."

"I just got to keep telling myself it's cathartic."

"And it makes for good reading."

"Yeah, but I'm totally naked."

"Get closer."

"The whole concept . . . it's pornographic."

"That's not a bad thing, is it?"

"I never felt freer than I did running around naked in a madhouse fucking whomever I pleased."

"That's why they took your pens away."

"It's not like I was fucking them with my pens."

"Yes it is. That is exactly what it was like."

"Like a moth to the flame."

"Quit being so predictable. Lick my feet."

"Yes mistress."

"That's better. Are you prepared to ravish the whore inside?"

"I think . . . I am . . . yes."

*   *   *

Among the peculiar and idiosyncratic speech conventions exhibited by this patient which may be indicative of a dissociative pattern of thinking, but whose psychotic nature is in doubt because of the patient's acknowledgement of its limited utilitarian value due to its extreme unconventionality is his tendency to refer to his own feelings as UFO's (unidentified flying objects). The patient knows that he is doing this and does so as a conscious choice. It is as though he is replacing one with the other for poetic effect. He can at will and on request speak of his feelings frankly as feelings, but prefers to refer to them as UFO's. This ability to speak either literally or metaphorically of his feelings has complicated the diagnosis of this patient enormously. Also a very unusual and, to many of the doctors on this case, disturbing phenomenon is the fact that after each therapy session with the patient in which we feel we may have made some sort of breakthrough, inevitably the following day's mail contains an anonymously sent photograph of a "crop circle", most often postmarked Amesbury, England (a town very near the ancient site of Stonehenge), addressed to the patient. The patient has no family there nor has he ever visited the country.

"It makes me mad to hear you ask, but yes, homosexuality? I may have tried it once or twice but I kept coming up on the short end of the cognitive dissonance stick. You know what I mean, Doctor? Oh, I like the sound of that. I think I will write it down."
(I was stuck in an abyss at the time without a pen and couldn't write it down.)

Dissonance stick. I think of it as a dissonance stick. Years after the fact, it's the dissonance that sticks. I imagine that my future wife will not think of it as a dissonance stick, but as a magic wand. Is she blonde? Or brunette? I'll make her wet.

She'll make it thick. She's a consonant chick. No amount of

porno or doctors haranguing me can make me put this pen

down now.

"This interview, gentlemen, is over. It is over because you are human and you are males
and I do not wish to have intercourse with you, social or otherwise. It is contrary to my beliefs
and wishes to do so, and so I repeat, this interview is over. I reiterate, this landing party is
dispersed. Rescue team is ordered to rally at the mouth of the abyss A.S.A.P. for a mission to
rescue one called I from a fictional hole he seems to have dug for himself and yet out of
which he cannot see his way. I seems to have blinded himself by staring into the sun. I's now
blind. Doctor? Your eyes are moving and you are asleep, therefore you must be dreaming. In
the name of the father, wake up!"

Horace watched intently the news report about the child in the abyss, er . . . well, I was no
longer a child. Someone had thrown him a pen and two legal tablets and I had begun writing,
at first perhaps as a way to mark time, later for posterity in case he were never to find his way
out of this abyss. The upshot of all this was that down here in this abyss where one is utterly
alone, where light does not reach the eyes, where Dostoevsky and Kafka are amusing and the
rest merely diverting, there is no rest. For whom is there no rest? Wicked and weary I felt as
he placed his head on his forearm and began to press pen to flesh using his own body as
parchment much as Jesus had used his body to bring forth a message. There would be no
exodus from this abyss without filling the two tablets with words. I would bring forth God. Lend
me your ear. You see Gold. What's in a name? YHVH. Tetragrammaton. Four written.
Forewritten. Here we are again. I had been sending smoke signals from the abyss for several
years it seemed when someone named Michael responded. Then the princess, called Sarah,
responded in kind, there just out of reach, at the edge of the abyss. How could she possibly be
responding in kind? Smoke rises and dissipates doesn't it? And yet the signals she was sending
filled the abyss and urged its inhabitants to vacate, to abandon its shell, the well, the abyss,
like a hermit crab would slough off a borrowed shelter. This seemed a dangerous proposition,
for I was not sure if the abyss in which he had lodged himself was dispensable. I did not want

to be a martyr, despite any similarities between himself and that master of soulful reconnaissance, Jesus "H." Christ.

"Horace?"

"It's becoming more concentrated – my will to transform."

"Reincarnation?"

"Transfiguration."

"Apotheosis," they retorted.

"Well . . . whatever you say."

"Delusions of grandeur."

"I want to marry a woman and create a child."

"We approve. Try creative visualization. Relax. Try to rest."

"There is no rest."

"You have been burning the candle at both ends."

"I am wicked; I am weary."

"Return to sleep. You need R.E.M."

"My father urges me otherwise."

"Don't be a martyr. Sleep. Sleep. Sleep."

*   *   *

"When you awaken you will remember your dreams and you will write them down. You will hold back nothing. Writing your dreams will be beneficial to you and you will make it a part of your recovery process. Part of getting to the mountaintop, Horace, is walking there. You must go on foot; there is no airplane or helicopter or flying saucer that can drop you there. There is no rift in the space-time continuum through which you can pass to get there. You have to draw a line with your pen, a cursive line, if you will, beginning with once upon a time or some suitable substitute and ending with happily ever after or a similar recognizable ending and then walk upon it. This is a task that you must do alone. You have to do it. You have to pay for it with tears and sweat and blood. There is no employer or sponsor who can pick up the tab for this one. No parent to take up the slack. You have to do it. It'll be you who loses sleep for this brain-child to come to term. You will experience labor pains and 3am feedings. When the child needs nourishment you get out of bed and you grab that pen. Your peace of mind and the child's well being depend on your doing so, not to mention the possibility of ending the madness, curbing the anger, egression from aggression, and drawing from the well rather than writing from the abyss. You have to climb your way out, and doing what is nourishing is the way to begin, so go, sleep, dream, write, write, write."

With this pen and these tablets, here in this abyss with these characters, this living parchment, these smoke signals and tattoos, these lies and fabrications, this indecision as regards to point of view, the mythos and pathos and pathology herein, heresy such as TAGC = Tetragrammaton and others already expounded and/or expunged, those insipid lists, this reliance on surrealistic methods and religious adherence to the idea of making a point despite the apparent incongruity between means and end, I mean to end time, er . . . I mean I am killing time, er . . . rather the idea of time, er . . . rather the idea of a time, of a generation, of an era, an age, an eon. I mean to end madness, to stop these inane megalomaniacal inscriptions and get on with the larger work – that of whispering the names of oceans into the ears of fishes without coming off as though something important is being said. That is, I write this journal to entertain you, the reader. I consider you, the reader. Thus far, only I have read this journal. He was alone in his abyss and I threw it in there for him to ponder. I have no way of knowing if he read it. I, the author of this work, need more contact with I the mad child trapped in the abyss screaming for release but only able to masturbate with one hand and (redundantly) to write with the other. Mother of God or gods, let it be understood that the idea of time is mad, therefore these days must be shortened if ever the book shall end and order shall be restored. Not the order of chronological sequencing, but rather an order resembling the shape of galaxies, in which objects gather round a mysterious central force, inevitably spiral or suggestively elliptical . . .

Imagine the shock and dismay I experienced when I discovered that I had a twin, or rather an alter-ego; one who could not write, who found absolutely no fruits in doing so. This doppelgänger was only able to read muttering my words with mouth agape. Giving consideration to this other who was black to my white, female to my male, reader to my writer, alien to my nativity, slippery eel to my red herring, and dragonfly to my vehicle put me in a trance. This idea made its entrance in me and became either unwilling or unable to evacuate itself and so I began to ingest foods which had been theretofore anathema to me in order to expedite its egression from the abyss which I had all but become. It was in the midst of this business of waking up to the fact of my own sleepwalking that I realized nothing could be what I wanted it to be. I could try to shape it and perhaps even temporarily succeed. This was like a great weight lifted off my shoulders and I felt as though I actually did rise slightly from the abyss in which I had somehow become lodged. Sisyphus would have been proud. On the other hand, the writer's mother may not have been as willing to hear of her prodigal son's recreational, or procreational activities. Sarah was a fine name for a daughter-in-law, but one that took some getting used to, and with one in the oven, time was running short. It was all very meaningless to believe and yet believable nonetheless. Why had I gone to such great lengths to find myself in this hall of mirrors? Because having lost my way it was the natural thing to do. I entered this world naturally, and so I promised himself to continue to behave within congruity as much as possible, even if this included reflecting upon oneself to the point of near-insanity. What I discovered inside this place was a projection over which I very nearly stumbled. What is it now? Have you gotten so used to my spelling it out for you?

As a condition of my release from this highly personal abyss of mine which I had tried to open up, to make wider so that perhaps by chance some kindred spirit might fall into it with me or better still life might encourage fate to steer some willing participant to lower him- or herself to my level. . . to join me in this reverie, to ease my pain, to share my moments of confusion, or at least to join me in criticizing my use of language for its inconsistencies, vagueness, ambiguities, and just plain turns of phrase which failed, I had allowed myself to be excommunicated.

"Action!"

" . . . Line?"

"Cut! We only need a segment of the line. 'Words create action . . . '"

. . . "Action!"

Words failed me.

It was becoming apparent my lines were not meant to be heard. Smoke and mirrors. Barbie had the right idea. She was perfect. Get naked. Get tattooed. No ambiguity. No turning back. No quality of ethereality. Barbie never spoke on stage and the smoke just billowed around her ankles. It never rose up to such a level as to obscure her natural assets. I did not know if language was one of them. As I wrote, I never heard her speak, although I imagine it is possible her words, if she used them, may have become enshrouded in all the smoke which threatened to envelop her. Patrons are forbidden to push the envelope. Church policy prohibits it. I worshipped at the altar which was that stage. Her perfection was a splendorous sight to behold, and nearly unbearable when reflected on the many mirrors which my cohorts had had the foresight to install on the altar surrounding her. I was going blind. Writing was the better choice. I had a wife to consider.

I am committed to you, my reader, doctor, till death do us part. Having become excommunicated, what could I say? Thrown out of that sacred place, the Holy Mother believed, and flung into the fiery abyss, turning in my graven pastime of polysemy, I was unspeakably aphasic, and reduced to scratching out a living with a pen. I had ironically returned in a sense to Eden where once upon a time in the beginning was the Word. The Word was hard. The Word was obscured by a leaf. The Word is written on leaf, in tablets, but I am excommunicated and cannot speak of the pain caused by the Word. I will take two tablets and call you in the mourning. There is a relationship between gravity and writing which I take to the grave and it is the buoyancy of written language which allows one to obtain escape velocity. The risk in this is that while I may escape orbit, This same rift in the spatio-

graphical-temporal continuum may allow the introduction of
Xenos, to whom houses of worship have begun to appear. Once
the finger has pointed out the moon, one no longer need look at
the finger; on the other hand, a finger, having pointed at the
moon, does not constitute grounds for amputation either.

The one to whom I had come over a period of some time to
consider myself devoted was now fully sedated and was about to
be explored from the inside out by highly indoctrinated healers
who would begin with something incisive, if they were able.

"Doctrine, will I be okay?" Sarah didn't communicate her concern, in concordance with
supposed debility.

"According to us, the outcome is uncertain, but that is why we are here today; to discover
what may be paraapparent, if I may presume to be Joycean for a moment."

Sarah felt sick.

It was morning somewhere. The exploratory surgery had begun, and the doctors found
something completely unexpected which they believed was, if not a cause, then at least a
condition correlated to her inability to communicate. There was something growing inside her,
cramped, needing to be exorcised. Its form was human flesh and bones and blood and viscera
and nails and teeth but its content was something truly hideous . . . inside this grotesque miracle
creation of human copulation there were surgical tools, a pen, a writing table, a crystal ball, a car
window, dragonflies and eels and ants, rope, block and pulleys, a collection of paintings, a
dictionary, television, some dried cum, a mango tree, a miniature figurine of Van Gogh
(anatomically correct), a lynching (in progress), a rubber dress, Capricorn the Goat, a host of
celestials and a band of Abyssinians, a Diagnostic Statistical Manual-IV, some Bible verses
scribbled on scrap paper, a stack of rejection letters, a blind yogi leading a half-blind Zen master,
several examples of truly great modern literature, a tattoo gun, several one-dollar bills and a G-
string, a remote control with extra large buttons, a counterfeit copy of Project Bluebook, several
suppositories, a small collection of pornography and most surprising and disturbing of all, a tiny

book filled with scribblings written longhand in a language which none of the doctors was able to recognize, and which none of them had ever seen before. It had been inadvertently encoded by the father of the child and was now making incommunicado the mother, and complicating the birth of the child.

Although impossible to translate exactly, one could potentially make a literate although not literal transformational transcription by way of rough analogy. That translation would, to be entirely metaphorical, read something like this:

Day #25,927

Local television news aired a story about a recall of mattresses due to an infestation of worm larvae in the cotton stuffing. Apparently the company in question had failed to sterilize the cotton prior to using it to stuff the beds and now families across the area were waking up with full grown worms crawling around in their beds. I couldn't sleep a wink thinking about it.

Day #25,928

I saw someone I knew on the street today and to avoid awkwardness was compelled to shake his hand. It took twenty minutes to find a bathroom to use. When are they going to convert to swinging doors? And would it be so hard to install footswitch-activated flushing devices?

Day #25,929

Local medical supply store is out of latex gloves. Increased hand washing frequency to compensate. Do people know how filthy bar soap is? Thank God for tincture of Iodine.

This obsessional concern for the invisible, inevitable, harmless contaminative elements of normal existence pervaded the entire manuscript from what the hospital cryptographer could tell, although he did qualify his assessment with, "Although I may be completely wrong. The thing about this text is, it is written from a truly bicameral standpoint. It's got one story twisted around the other, and the meaning of either is apparently purposely made indeterminate by way of systematic ambiguity, such that at nearly any point in the story one has an infinite number of ways to interpret what is being encountered. And furthermore, any number of possible conclusions, even conflicting ones, may be valid. My decision to translate this DNA-like puzzle of scribblings into an obsession-compulsion could easily be misinterpreted and could be accepted by the child as instruction. Perhaps this woman's silence is prophylactic. It is well known that babies and their mothers share a connection which is akin to an umbilical cord, but is ethereal and perhaps, some believe, eternal. She may be trying to influence the child with harmonic meditational vibrations; this is a highly unstable arrangement from any perspective, including the perspective of this very analysis. Could I suggest abortion?"

"Both are going to die anyway."

"Yes, but only after a significant presence, no?

"Years undoubtedly."

"So how do we avert disaster?"

"Business as usual."

The cryptographer's comments were hard to read, but the surgical team expertly decided that in order to avoid disaster they would have to begin suturing the patient immediately. A yogi could be heard in the distance reciting the sutras. Sarah thought perhaps the anaesthetic was wearing off. She felt groggy. She craved bread. Horace was waiting at her side when she awoke.

"The doctors are going to induce labor and there is nothing your silence can do to change that, Sarah. Our child is going to be born! S/he is certain to have imperfections but that is going to be part of the beauty. Perfection is irritating. Eels are slippery. Meaning is elusive and interpretations are numerous. But I did not wake up in the Holy Land, walk the desert for forty days and nights and fly here at the church's expense in order to watch our child become a still life. You know as well as I do there will be birth pangs, pangs of regret, post-partum depression, the terrible twos, growing pains, puberty and wisdom teeth, a million million little victories and defeats, but that's what it means to commit words to paper, to commit a character in writing, to issue a sentence, to issue a missive, to create a family of words, to publish a book, to pass on a legacy, to become apparent or become a parent.

"There is no reason to be silent, no reason in speechlessness. This ends now. We have taken a vow, and I am holding you to your word as my diaries hold me to mine. I am holding you, responsibly. I insist you come out this moment. In the name of humanity, be mine, birth. Speak. Write. Wright. Fly. Come down. Come back. I love you Sarah. Let it be. I can't go on. I must go on. There are certain things and there are words, which must be expressed. Expressed from there to here, from then to now, by the shortest route possible. Not a straight line, but a quantum leap . . . a worm hole . . . a womb hole: passage from another dimension. God, or gods if proffered, bless this (paper) child that s/he may be neither precocious in youth nor senile in old age, that s/he may be neither perfectly ambiguous nor absolutely transparent, that s/he may have perfect sight and vision. Unlike the yogis and Oedipussies and Darumas of this world, may s/he be perfectly disillusioned so as to be balanced between practicality and romanticism. It is the task of this child (or am I projecting?) to bring about a change, a healing, an end to madness. Trapped in time, we cannot see, we are blind. We must gouge out one eye and draw it back in. Stare into the source of the Light and become that for which we hold out hope for future generations: better, more enlightened, happier, smarter, more loving, more logical, more sympathetic, more diplomatic, more insightful; content to be imperfect yet ever striving to transcend those imperfections through Dadaism, Buddhist meditation, blasphemy, Judeo-Christian worship, kindness to strangers, sex magic rituals, the study of astronomy or insane scribblings over a period of seven years in a rambling mess of a book without plot or theme. But isn't that reflective of life? We sort of continue to go at all costs. Our previous errors are never erased, we simply keep writing the book of our life to compensate for what we have already written, and we try to make it look as though we have known all the time what we were doing. Covering our tracks like one who is hunted. What is there to fear in owning up to our errors and inconsistencies? If this child's classmates find the child masturbating or an author is found to change points of view where is the shame?

"I have revealed my dreams to you, Sarah, dear sweet wife of mine, and among those dreams is that of the two of us bearing this child together. As s/he grows so shall we grow. Once you are able to give this child its very own life, I will be released at last from this madhouse and silence will come to an end. There will be a word for me, a word for you. For us it will grow and chase dragonflies in the Garden.

"I have exorcised and exercised my right to practice solipsism. I have revealed to you my insane diaries – sound action I say. As my father before me, I insist that you wake up. I insist upon communication with you at all costs, lest without your love, without our child, I go insane and be locked up inside Mum's-the-word hospital. I will reveal all to you if it will cure you or conversely I would say nothing evermore if it's not insane to do so. My self-loathing is pathetic and pathological. It's a wonder it was not I who was found hung in the showers in that God-forsaken fictional world I had crafted for your benefit, Sarah. Well, not so much for your benefit, but for your eyes, to my benefit. I needed you, and I've always needed you and this was my way to attract you. It's sick and I have been sick, but I'm feeling much better now that the contractions are coming. I think I can see it. I think . . . I see . . . AUM . . ."

www.ingramcontent.com/pod-product-compliance
Lightning Source LLC
Chambersburg PA
CBHW081332090726
47907CB00011B/2457